The Christmas Cookie Conundrum

A Pinewood Corners Sweet Romance

CAROL BABINEAUX

THE CHRISTMAS COOKIE CONUNDRUM
A Pinewood Corners Sweet Romance

Book Design by
Transcendent Publishing
www.transcendentpublishing.com

Edited by Lori Lynn

ISBN: 979-8-9890682-0-3

Printed in the United States of America.

Dedication

For Michael, whose love and support enabled
me to create this book.

Table of Contents

Chapter 1

"**M**ichaela! Where are the extra trays of rolls I ordered from you?"

Startled out of an upright doze, my elbow slipped off the counter and jarred me awake. "Coming right up, Stefan!"

I rushed over to the ovens along the wall and managed to get the trays of rolls out just in time to keep them from over-baking. As I slid the trays into the cooling rack, I breathed a sigh of relief mixed with chagrin.

Two years of culinary arts schooling with a focus on baking and pastry, not to mention all the student loan baggage, so I could spend my days making endless trays of dinner rolls in the kitchens of the Madison House Resort. I had wanted so much more for myself.

When I graduated from culinary school, I had dreams beyond the monotony of making rolls. I wanted to make people happy with my baking creations. Rolls don't really make anyone that happy, they just sit in a basket on the table as placeholders before the "real" meal arrives. With all the carb-phobia these days, most of my rolls ended up in the trash bin.

My big, bold, secret dream, the one that I didn't even dare to speak aloud, was that I would someday be able to run my very own bakery. I longed to have the independence of being an entrepreneur, managing my own time and deciding what I would bake and sell each day in my shop.

I would publish cookbooks of my best baking creations and make even more people happy because people would be able to use my recipes to make their loved ones happy, too. For me, baking equaled joy.

But I wasn't finding any joy in my job, so I stayed up nights baking cookies to post on my social media pages. I offered my custom-decorated cookies for sale to small catered events like wedding showers and office parties.

I did find joy in making my own creations, but the schedule was killing me. When I wasn't working, I was baking or doing delivery and setting up my custom cookie orders. I was probably getting 30 to 35 hours of sleep in a good week.

I knew I couldn't keep up this pace, but I didn't have enough business to support myself with my cookie catering. Plus, I had those student loans to pay. So I had to stay at the Madison House Resort and make sure my kitchen manager was adequately supplied with rolls.

"Michaela! The rolls!" Stefan shouted. "Get them off the racks and into the baskets! We have full tables tonight. After you get these off the trays, start another batch." He threw the towel he was carrying over his shoulder and raised his bushy eyebrows at me.

"Sure, Stefan, right away." I felt like Bill Murray's character in *Groundhog Day,* reliving the same actions over and over again. Or maybe in my case, life was more like the old Dunkin' Donuts commercials, with the "time to make the donuts" guy: a haggard baker on such a repetitive schedule that he literally ran into himself coming and going, endlessly making donuts. I could definitely relate.

Stefan looked somewhat mollified. "And tuck your hair into your hat! I don't need any health violations in my kitchen."

I self-consciously shoved my long side-bangs behind my ear and pulled my baker's cap lower. My fine light brown hair was wavy with a tendency to frizz; it had a mind of its own and was always trying to assert itself.

I washed my hands and turned to the baking trays with a sigh. "Time to make the donuts," I muttered.

*   *   *

It was after midnight when I got in my car to go home. Before pulling away, I waved to Stefan, who had walked me out to my car. I turned on the wipers to remove the thin layer of slush on the windshield and cranked up the heater.

"Hey Siri, play my voicemails," I said. My phone obliged by telling me I had three new messages. One was a co-worker asking to trade shifts over the weekend. One was a robo-call telling me that my car warranty was in imminent jeopardy of expiring. The last message was from my Grandma Jo. Hearing her voice cheered me up a little after my long night of work.

"Mikki, hi!" she chirped, using my childhood nickname. "I hope you're planning to come home for this year's Lights by the Lake holiday festival. I sure miss you, my girl."

I almost stopped the playback at that point. I loved my grandma, but I hadn't been excited to attend my small hometown's annual holiday festival since I was a teen. Pinewood Corners indulged in all the usual Christmas excesses like holiday decorating competitions, a tree lighting ceremony at the town square, an ice-skating rink with piped-in carols, mistletoe over every doorway … the works. I hadn't felt the Christmas spirit in years. I was too darned tired. But because I loved my grandma, I gritted my teeth and let the message play on.

"There's lots of excitement this year," Grandma Jo's voice continued. "The annual holiday cookie bake off has attracted the attention of the Culinary Channel, and they want to film the competition. They're even offering a grand prize of *fifty thousand dollars*! I'll bet you could win that hands down, honey. Anyway, I know you're working and you can't talk, but call me back when you have a chance so we can gossip about all the juicy details. Love you, my girl."

A horn blasted as the car behind me pulled around on my left side and roared past. I realized that I had slowed far below the speed limit. My mind was racing, though. *Fifty thousand dollars, and a chance to be on a competition televised by the*

Culinary Channel. It felt like some fairy godmother had heard my wishes and waved a wand that could give me a chance to live the life of my wildest, most far-out dreams. In a daze, I pressed harder on the gas pedal and headed for home.

*   *   *

I unlocked the door to my apartment and draped my jacket over the faded easy chair in my living room. I referred to my decorating style as "cozy chic," but it was really a bunch of recycled thrift store finds. I wished I could say it was because I socked every extra penny away for my future bakery, but the truth was that there *were* no extra pennies.

Even with grabbing most of my meals from work, every cent I currently earned went towards the roof over my head, chipping away at my student loan debt, keeping my beater Chevy running, and feeding my cat. Said cat came ambling into the living room with a yawn and a stretch and meowed plaintively at me.

"Hello, Acorn." I bent and gave the gray tabby a scratch on his head. He purred appreciatively and rubbed against my hand. Even though I knew his affectionate greeting was motivated more by his joy at seeing his source of food rather than by my sparkling personality, it was still nice to be welcomed home.

I dumped a can of wet food into his bowl, topped off his dry food, and refreshed his water before turning to my own needs. I unwrapped the foil parcel I had brought home with me. Slices of tender roast beef with a cup of rich gravy on the side and chunks of golden roasted potatoes—no rolls, thank you very much.

"What do you think goes better with beef and potatoes, the raspberry or the coconut La Croix?" I asked Acorn. He looked up from his food briefly.

"Right," I said, "the tart notes of the raspberry will pair better with the richness of the beef." I grabbed the can of sparkling water from the door of the fridge and settled down with my late dinner and the remote. I found myself searching for baking shows on the Culinary Channel.

I watched the contestants running back and forth, grabbing ingredients, anxiously peering into the bowls of stand mixers, mopping sweaty brows with the backs of their wrists, wielding piping bags with shaking hands, and thanking the judges for both eviscerating and praising their work. *Can I do it? Do I really have what it takes?*

*   *   *

I glanced at my phone and saw that it was after 2 a.m. I clicked off the television and pitched the trash from my dinner. "Dishes are done," I told Acorn, leaning down to give him a pat. "Ready to go to sleep?"

He replied with a feline burble that I took as an affirmative response as he followed me down the short hall to the bedroom. Acorn immediately hopped onto my old brass bed and curled up on the intricate pink, green, and white flowered quilt that my Grandma Jo had made for me as a high school graduation present.

I headed to the sink in the adjoining bathroom to wash up for bed. I stared at myself in the bathroom mirror. My hair was bound back in a braid, my skin too pale, sallow and shiny, my hazel eyes too red and weary. The deep circles under my eyes looked even more purple and pronounced under the harsh fluorescent light from over the mirror. I seemed to be older than my 29 years by a decade. I knew in my heart that I had to make a change because I couldn't go on forever like this.

I shook myself out of my melancholy, brushed my teeth, and washed my face. I climbed into bed and arranged myself around Acorn as best I could. It was beyond me how an eight-pound cat could take up half the queen-sized bed. As I settled into the pillows, I stared up at the ceiling, worrying and thinking.

It would cost me dearly to miss two weeks of work over the holidays, not to mention foregoing any holiday cookie orders for my side business if I decided to go home and enter the bake off. But if I passed up this opportunity, it might cost me far more than money. If I won, the prize money and the exposure would give my culinary career a tremendous boost. I sighed and rolled over. Acorn grunted and flipped onto his back, legs in the air.

"Acorn, should I do this? *Can* I do this?"

He snored softly in response.

My mind whirled. I had a small emergency fund saved up and a few good pieces of jewelry that I could sell if it came down to needing funds to cover the next couple of weeks. But it was nerve-wracking to consider giving up my meager safety net.

Eventually, I fell asleep and dreamed that I was being attacked by giant gingerbread-man cookies while a panel of judges looked on and gave me constructive criticism.

I awoke to Acorn on my chest, kneading his claws into my pajama top.

"Ow," I mumbled and rolled over. "Okay, okay, I'm up."

I grabbed my phone from the nightstand to check the time. I was grateful that I didn't have to rush a cookie order to an event and I could relax a bit and enjoy a slow morning. I got out of bed to make some coffee and get going with my day.

First on the agenda was calling my Grandma Jo back to get the "juicy details" as she put it. She answered on the first ring.

"Mikki!" she cried, the delight shining in her voice as I put the phone on speaker. "How's everything in the big city?"

I laughed. "Grandma, Wilton is hardly the big city; it's a moderately large tourist town." I pushed the plunger down on my French press. The earthy scent of the fresh-ground Sumatran dark coffee beans washed over me. My brain cells started sparking to life as I inhaled deeply. Good coffee was the one luxury I allowed myself.

"Well, to a born and bred small-town gal like me, anything with more than three stoplights is a big city," Grandma Jo replied.

I could hear the familiar squeak-slam of her storm door and figured that she had been out filling the bird feeder in her yard as she usually did every morning.

"How are the tufted titmice?" I asked her.

"Darn squirrels keep trying to chase everybody off," she groused.

I laughed again, picturing her scowling as I poured coffee into my favorite mug that bore the slogan "Bakers Rise to the Occasion." I added a dollop of French vanilla creamer, stirring the swirling clouds with a spoon, and sipped. *Sheer heaven.*

"Grandma, what's this about the holiday festival? The Culinary Channel really is coming? It isn't just a rumor that Mayor Reese started to drum up more interest?"

"No!" Grandma Jo replied emphatically. "I saw the network executives myself! They came up here in big black fancy SUVs and they marched into the mayor's office and met with him for a whole day."

"I'll bet everyone in town suddenly had business to take care of on Main Street that day, including you," I teased.

"You know it," Grandma Jo said with a hearty chuckle. "Folks like to think they know what's what—and spread their knowledge around."

"Grandma, that's the best euphemism for being nosy and gossiping that I've ever heard."

"Of course Rayna thinks she's a shoo-in, even though everyone knows that half the time she tries to pass off sugar cookies from the Fresh Stop as her own," she said, referring to Mayor Reese's daughter.

I rolled my eyes, remembering how Rayna—beautiful and rich and mean—had loved embarrassing me in high school by taping notes to my back, planting toilet paper for me to step on and trail all over campus, starting vicious rumors about me

… even "tripping" and spilling her lunch tray all over me in the crowded cafeteria.

"Isn't there a conflict of interest with her entering or something?" I asked.

"I don't reckon so," Grandma Jo replied, "I understand anyone can enter so long as you or your immediate family don't work for the Culinary Channel. They're supplying all the judges."

"You should enter, Grandma. Your cookies are the best."

"I don't believe it, but I sure love to hear it," Grandma Jo said. "Besides, I'm leaving the spot for you. Registration opened first thing this morning, and I guarantee it's going to fill up fast. Everybody in town who's ever made a Betty Crocker cake mix thinks they've got a chance."

"Thanks, Grandma. Definitely something to think about."

"What's to think about? I signed you up already, easy-peasy." My grandmother sounded satisfied.

"You what!?" I cried, shocked. "I have bills, I have a job, I have to think about the logistics involved," I started to protest.

"Honey," she said softly, "It's much easier to talk yourself out of your wildest dreams, but that won't get you anywhere. Cover your shifts and come on home. I have enough faith in you and your talents that I've paid the entry fee already."

"You did *what?* Grandma, that's wonderful and generous, but you shouldn't have—"

"Nonsense," Grandma Jo cut off my protest. "It's a worthy investment."

I thought about my schedule for a moment.

"I suppose there's time to get my shifts covered at the resort. But my cookie orders—"

"Well, when should I expect you? Your room is all ready and I'm working on my grocery list. You still like baked macaroni and cheese topped with bacon bits and bread crumbs, right?"

I closed my eyes. I hadn't had that dish in years, and it sounded way too rich for my adult palate, but I couldn't bear to hurt my grandma's feelings, so I said, "You bet!" And that's when I knew that I was definitely going back home for the holidays.

Chapter 2

Grandma Jo had a tendency to exaggerate. Pinewood Corners actually possessed six stoplights and a plethora of four-way stop sign intersections.

I pulled up to the first of the town's stoplights and took the opportunity to glance around. Things hadn't changed too much since I had left. The atmosphere was still as rustic and charming as ever. The brisk air even carried the familiar scent of pine and woodsmoke.

A huge banner advertising the upcoming annual holiday festival stretched over the intersection. Accented by sprigs of pine boughs intertwined with red berries and crystal lights, it would twinkle merrily at night.

The holiday festival was a big tradition in Pinewood Corners, going way back to when trapper and merchant Merrick McKenna had founded the town. Legend has it, McKenna was ready to settle down, so he sent away for a bride from Ireland. His bride, Maeve, had become lonely and homesick and unhappy in her new life. Wishing to cheer up his wife,

McKenna had devised a holiday festival for her to organize. She had loved it so much that she continued the tradition every year up until her disappearance. After that, the McKenna's children kept it up, until it had become a part of the town long after the McKenna family tree faded from town leadership.

In fact, Pinewood Corners was known as a "festival town" in the region. In addition to the Lights by the Lake festival, there was the Sweetheart Soiree in February, the Spring Swing in April, the Sunshine Celebration in June, Dog Days in August, and Harvest Happenings in late October/early November.

The town also featured a spectacular farmers market in the town square every weekend from May through September, which showcased local artisans and craftspeople as well as seasonal produce and local honey.

All the festivals and the farmers market had kept the town's blood pumping, attracting visitors from all around to shop and enjoy the festivities. Many of the tourists decided to stay on for multiple days, booking into the local inns and bed-and-breakfast establishments in town.

"Mrrwowww!" came a plaintive cry from the carrier on my passenger seat.

"I know, Acorn, poor kitty. It's awful how you're being treated. Don't worry, I'm sure Grandma Jo has a kitty stocking full of toys and treats and catnip waiting for you."

The light turned green, but as I pulled through the intersection, I noticed a patrol car pulling up behind me. In a flash of red and blue, I guided my old Chevy to the curb. I observed an older man getting out of the police car, hatless, with steel gray hair and a still-slender build. He was smiling as he approached my car window.

"Hey, Mikki, welcome home!" Sheriff Bob Weaver had been the sheriff of Pinewood Corners since I could remember. He was a kind-hearted man who had tolerated most of the teenage antics that my friends and I had gotten in to in the past, and I had always liked him. "I thought that was you at Greener's Gas Station, so I had to stop you to say hello!"

"Hi, Sheriff," I replied. "Thanks. It's nice to be home for the holidays. You're looking good. Life must be treating you well these days."

"Thanks, Mikki, no complaints here," he said with a smile. "Headed out to your grandma's place?" Without waiting for me to answer, he continued, "Great lady, your grandma. I think you'll find the town has been growing since you left. I had to hire on a deputy this year, especially with all the extra folks expected with the festival this Christmas and all that hub-bub with the TV food people. You remember Tom, Tom Willis? He's Deputy Willis now. Doing a great job of it, too, I'm pleased to say. I'll need someone to take over for me when I retire." He finally stopped to take a breath.

"Sheriff, you're in your prime," I told him. He was probably 70 if he was a day, but he was such a fixture in town that I couldn't imagine Pinewood Corners without him.

He waved away my compliment. "Well, enjoy your visit. Tell your grandma hey for me, and tell her that I sure enjoyed the cherry cobbler she made." He smiled broadly at me. "I'd better get going. No telling what folks are getting up to out there." The Sheriff pulled a pair of mirrored aviator sunglasses from his shirt pocket and slipped them on. With a bob of his head, he climbed into his patrol car and pulled around me with a wave and a whoop of his siren.

I chuckled to myself as I navigated my car back onto the road. It was nice to be welcomed back to town but a little disconcerting to be pulled over. Luckily I was still near the outskirts of town, or the gossip mill would've been in full swing. I glanced around as I drove farther into town, trying to reorient myself to my old stomping grounds.

As a matter of fact, I did remember Tom Willis. We had dated briefly in high school when I was a shy sixteen-year-old and he was a worldly man of seventeen. We would sit next to each other during movies, my sweaty hand holding his. When I passed him in the hallway at school, I would slip a handwritten note into his hand with a coy smile. All of that came to an end when he graduated from Pinewood High School and moved away to attend college.

It was good to know he was back in town. I found myself wondering idly if he was still single, until I remembered that I had goals and dreams to pursue and no time for rekindling old flames.

I drove on and passed Marcus Pharmacy, the sandwich shop, and Crawford's Hardware. I noticed a few new businesses—an antique store, a health food store, and a cute little coffeehouse among them.

Main Street was decked out with glittering strands of white lights, pine wreaths festooned with bright red velvety ribbons hanging from the street lamps, and picturesque mounds of snow lingering in the shady spots of the sidewalks as if they had been planted there by a decorating committee. Banners across the top of the road, linked between the quaint old-fashioned lights made to look like Victorian era gas street lamps, advertised the annual Lights by the Lake holiday festival that would begin in a few days.

The merchants had begun setting up their holiday window displays. The competition was fierce for the title of "Most Spirited Decor" amongst the shopkeepers in Pinewood Corners. The prize was awarded by the Merchant's Association and included a writeup in the local paper and a framed certificate that was displayed with pride at the winner's business all year long.

I turned off onto the little lane just past the last four-way stop. The handmade sign proclaimed the roadway "Sugarplum Lane." My grandfather had made the sign himself, naming the private lane after his nickname for me when I was a toddler. Because he had passed on when I was very small, I had only dim memories of him.

*   *   *

My grandma had taken care of me during every school year of my life since I was six years old, all the way through high school. I was an only child, and my parents eked out a very modest living as actors, traveling all over the country with their theater troupe. They didn't think it was fair to drag me around all the time, so my grandma's house was the only real stability that I'd had as a child. She was the reason that I loved baking so much. Grandma Jo's cookies, warm from the oven, always made me feel safe and happy and loved.

She must have been watching out the window for me. As soon as my car pulled into the carport, my grandma came out the side door. Grinning from ear to ear, she greeted me with arms open wide. "Mikki!" she shrieked and pulled me into her embrace. She smelled like lavender and vanilla, just like always.

"Hi Grandma." My voice sounded muffled against the fluffy chenille sweater she wore. As she pulled back, I saw that the sweater was bright red with deep green around the collar and cuffs and displayed the portrait of a cartoon reindeer on the front, complete with a flashing red light for a nose. I held back a laugh. "Corny as ever," I said as I gestured to her sweater.

"You're a sight for sore eyes, sweetheart, but you look so, so—beige." She flapped her hands up and down, gesturing at my plain jeans and brown boots, and my hat, coat and scarf in varying shades of brown. "Where's your Christmas spirit?"

"I guess I misplaced it." I shrugged. "Help me get Acorn into the house and get him settled. I need to unpack and go get checked in for the bake off."

"I'm so glad you've decided to do this." Grandma Jo reached for Acorn's carrier, cooing to him about what a good, brave kitty he was. "You'd better get down there quick. The bake off is in less than a week!"

"I know. I called in every favor I had at work to get two weeks off at Christmas time. It's a busy time at the resort." Two unpaid weeks off. Not to mention that I'd had to post on social media that I would be unavailable for any cookie catering for two weeks over the holidays, which was prime cookie time. Mentally squaring my shoulders, I shook off my apprehension. Sometimes you have to make sacrifices and take risks in life, and this was one of those times.

I hauled my old battered suitcase out of the trunk and followed behind my grandmother into the house, which was decked out with strands of multi-colored lights on the eaves and around the bushes.

"By the way, I ran into Sheriff Weaver. He said hello and told me to tell you that he enjoyed the cherry cobbler."

Grandma Jo's cheeks flushed prettily. "Oh, that rascal! He'd better bring my dish back." Grandma pushed the side door open with her foot. "Get back, Napoleon!" she shouted at the little brown and white terrier whose snuffling head poked enthusiastically through the opening.

I looked around at the beloved and familiar living room, so cozy with the overstuffed furniture and the hearthfire burning merrily. One of Grandma Jo's cheerful quilts in shades of blue and cream was draped over the back of the couch. I wanted to curl up under it and enjoy the fire, but I had things to take care of before the day ended.

"What, no tree?" I asked my grandmother, feigning shock. "I expected nothing less than a six-foot Douglas fir decked out with strands of sparkling lights and weighed down with dozens of ornaments."

Grandma Jo laughed. "Not yet. I thought you and I could go to the tree lot tomorrow and pick out a nice tree and we could decorate it together."

"That would be lovely," I told her. I didn't really want to take the time away from practicing my bake off recipe, but I realized that it meant a lot to my grandma, and I didn't want to disappoint her.

It took almost an hour to get Acorn and Napoleon reacquainted, although Acorn was still sticking to the tops of the furniture and giving the dog wary looks.

As soon as I felt like things were settled with canine and feline matters, I grabbed my coat and scarf. "Gotta run, Grandma. I'll be back in time for dinner." I kissed her cheek and headed out the door.

*   *   *

I borrowed Grandma Jo's Jeep, at her insistence that it could snow, because as she put it, my tires were "as bald as an eagle!" As I arrived at the huge tent just off the town square where the cookie bake off was being held, I saw a trailer parked in front with a banner: "Bake Off Headquarters."

The interior of the trailer was stuffy and overly warm, so I immediately loosened my scarf as I entered. There was a desk with a couple of chairs in front of it and another row of chairs along the wall by the door. A man was seated in front of the desk with his back to me, talking with the woman sitting behind the desk. His dark blond hair curled over the back of his collar. I couldn't help noticing that he had very broad shoulders.

I took a seat by the door, wincing as I stretched out my car-trip weary legs. The woman behind the desk glanced over and lifted her chin to me in acknowledgment. She didn't look familiar, so I figured that she had been hired by the Culinary Channel to manage the bake off registrants. I didn't have to wait long.

After about five minutes, the blond man stood, thanked the woman, and they shook hands across the desk. The woman handed him a thick packet. The man shrugged on his coat and turned around. His eyes were a brilliant crystal blue and seemed to look right through me as he rushed towards the door. A moment too late, I drew my feet back as I felt his shins come into contact with my heavy boots.

"Oof!" he cried, instinctively reaching out to brace himself as he pitched forward, papers spilling from his hands. As he gripped my shoulders, both of us nearly toppled to the floor. He smelled pleasantly masculine, of pine and musk and pipe smoke.

"Excuse me," I began saying.

"What are you thinking? Someone could get hurt!" The man's scowl emphasized the unshaven planes of his face and his high cheekbones, his stubble sparkling like flecks of gold. His dark blond brows drew together, and he huffed as he bent to gather his papers.

"Well!" I stammered, "I'm okay, thank you so much for asking."

His definitely blue eyes narrowed as he looked me up and down. "I assumed as much, since you're the one sitting down and tripping people." He gave me one last glare as he stood and yanked open the trailer's door.

"Hello, are you all right?" The woman behind the desk was standing up and looking concerned.

"I'm okay, thanks, just a little allergic to rudeness," I replied irritably as the door slammed. I hoped the man had heard me.

"What can I help you with? I'm afraid our bake off booths are all spoken for. The contest is very popular this year because it's being televised." The woman was pleasant, middle-aged, with pointed features and short red hair that cupped her oval-shaped head. Large, round tortoiseshell glasses dominated her small face. The nameplate on the desk said Cindy Jenkins.

"Oh, I've been registered already. I'm here to check in."

Cindy Jenkins sat back down behind her desk. "Name?" she asked, turning her eyes to the computer screen in front of her.

"Michaela Branson," I supplied as I sat in the chair vacated by the rude man. She tapped away for a moment, and a look of concern crossed her face.

"Can you please spell that name for me?" she asked. I did so, and after some more tapping, she continued to look confused.

"What's wrong? I have a confirmation email, and the receipt from my entry fee. My grandmother took care of it all. Would you like to see it?" I began rummaging around in my huge faux leather purse for the printouts of my registration emails. My heart was pounding, and I felt the sweat beading up on my forehead. *Why is it so hot in here?*

She squinted at her computer monitor and muttered, "How strange—."

"Aha!" I extracted the pages and waved them at Cindy across the desk. She took them, looked them over, turned to the computer and tapped on the keyboard again.

"Oh, I see you now," she said. I could have cried with relief. Cindy opened a drawer and removed a packet like the one she had given Prince Not-So-Charming earlier. She held it out to me and said, "Your booth number, contestant badge, and all rules and regulations are included in the packet. Your registration number is the same as your booth number. You may go into the tent right now to inspect your space and your basic supplies that were provided upon registration. All other supplies specific to your recipe will be provided by you. You may practice in the tent starting the day after tomorrow at 8 a.m. The tent will open next Friday morning at 9 a.m. for the initial round of official baking, and judging will commence the following Saturday at 10 a.m. Please make sure that you are always wearing your badge to enter the tent and during the time you're there. If you have any further questions, please see one of the concierges in the tent. I'll just need for you to sign this release to appear on the Culinary Channel's broadcast of the bake off." She handed me a clipboard and pen.

"Thank you so much." I scribbled my signature and grabbed the packet from Cindy after she shook my hand.

"Good luck!" I heard her call out as I practically ran out the door of the trailer.

*   *   *

After the suffocating heat of the trailer, the air outside was like a cold slap in the face, brutal but refreshing. The tent entrance was directly behind the trailer. The long white tent with its clear plastic windows and peaked roof reminded me of my favorite British baking competition show's set. I grinned as a shiver of excitement rolled through me. I hadn't felt this thrilled in a very long time, and it felt like water over parched earth.

As I passed through the opening, the plastic chemical smell of the tent canvas mixed with the homey scents of vanilla, butter, and sugar from the rows of the open kitchen stations. The air hummed with activity as crew members in red sweatshirts worked to set up the last of the booths. A tall, friendly-looking man with a shaved head approached me. Dressed in black pants and a black vest over a white shirt, he wore a lanyard around his neck with a tag that said "Concierge" in block letters.

I held up my new badge and smiled at him. "Hi, I'm a contestant. I just checked in." I gestured behind me in the direction of the trailer. "I'm booth 447."

"Welcome," the man said, leaning over to examine my badge number. He immediately looked concerned, his brows drawing together. He glanced around the tent and hesitated. "Miss, could you please wait here for a moment?" he asked me as he turned to rush towards the back corner of the tent. He stopped at a table and spoke with several people seated behind it, gesturing at me and at a booth along the side towards the rear of the tent.

Now it was my turn to be confused. The booth the concierge was pointing to had the number 447 above it, but it was already occupied. The man's back was to me, but I would recognize those broad shoulders and that dark blond hair anywhere. He was busily inspecting the contents of various cabinets and shelves. I trooped over to the booth and cleared my throat loudly. He turned around and his pale blue eyes widened in surprise and then immediately narrowed at the sight of me.

"You!" I cried. "Why are you in my booth?"

"Excuse me, what are *you* doing in *my* booth?" the blond man replied hotly. "I just confirmed my registration for this booth, number 447." He stuck his badge out and waved it in my face.

"Whoa," I said, stepping back and waving my own badge. "According to this, booth 447 was assigned to *me*, see that?" I tapped the badge authoritatively. "Michaela Branson, contestant number 447." I looped the lanyard with my badge around my neck and crossed my arms smugly.

"There's still one little problem," the man said through clenched teeth, "because booth 447 was assigned to *me*, contestant 447." He overly enunciated the syllables of his name in a patronizing tone: "*Mi-chael Bran-don.*"

"You don't have to speak to me as if I'm stupid," I said, as the harried looking concierge approached, accompanied by an older man carrying an electronic tablet and wearing a small scowl below his bushy gray mustache. His badge proclaimed him to be an officiant of the bake off.

"Excuse me, there seems to have been a mistake here," the older man said politely. "This booth was somehow double booked. I believe the names are so similar that the person assigning the booths likely mistook you for the same person."

"That's okay, mistakes happen," I told him. "I'll just take another booth."

"I'm afraid that's not possible," the man replied. "All the booths have been assigned already and we have no more room."

"Well, I checked in first, so the booth is mine." Michael Brandon planted his palms possessively on the countertop and gave me a challenging look.

"Oh no you don't," I cried. "When did you register? I registered a week ago!" In my agitation, I dumped my purse onto the counter, frantically searching for my printouts again. Lipstick, tubes of lotion and hand sanitizer, coins and mints and other purse clutter rolled around and over the edge of the counter and onto the floor. The concierge bent to retrieve the spilled items.

I waved the papers at the officiant. "See? I paid my fees and received confirmation and everything last week."

The officiant took the pages and examined them briefly before handing them back to me. He consulted his tablet, tapping and swiping around on the screen. "It appears that you both signed up eight days ago," he said as he adjusted his glasses. "According to the official rules," he continued, "the booths can be occupied by a single contestant or by a team of two. You cannot share a booth unless you are on a team. You may either decide which of you is willing to bow out, and then one of you can continue as a single contestant of this booth, and we will refund the entry fee to the other person, or you may continue together, as a team."

"What about the prize money?" I asked. "Is it doubled for a team?"

The officiant turned and looked at me as if I had lost my marbles. "Certainly not. The prize money is the same regardless of being a single or team winner. You would obviously share the winnings."

"Obviously," Michael said dryly, "I'm not bowing out."

"Me neither!" I sounded like a stubborn six-year-old, even to myself, but I was infuriated. My dreams were on the line, and I was prepared to do anything to preserve my chance at making them come true. Anything, no matter how crazy it sounded. Even teaming up with this total jerk.

The jerk glared at me, his face reddening. "No way I'm working with *her*. She tripped me earlier, trying to eliminate her competition, but I won't give up that easily."

"That was an accident!" I said indignantly. "You should learn to watch where you're going!"

"You should keep your feet to yourself!"

"Maybe you would see better if you'd pull your head out of your—"

"Please, people, *please* stop this pointless arguing," the officiant interjected. "If you cannot come to a rational decision based on the choices given to you, I will be forced to disqualify you both immediately."

I stopped short and looked at Michael, my hazel eyes locking with his pale blue ones. His face red, his lips compressed, he shrugged, grudgingly and almost imperceptibly. I raised my eyebrows in an inquiring "Are you sure?" gesture. Michael bobbed his head, looking pained. I took a deep breath and plunged in. "We'll take it!"

The officiant looked confused. "Take what?" he asked.

"The booth, we'll take the booth. I mean, we'll take it together, as a team." It wasn't the situation I would have chosen, but at least I still had a chance.

"Do you agree, Mr. Brandon?" the officiant inquired, turning to Michael.

Michael looked as if he would rather put his foot into a meat slicer than work with me, but he was probably thinking along the same lines as me: any chance at winning was better than no chance. With a sigh, he said, "Yes, fine, I agree, as long as it keeps me in the competition."

"Very well, then. I will need your team name by the end of business tomorrow," the officiant said, typing something on his tablet. He strode away as the concierge trailed after him.

I turned to Michael. "Well, it looks like we're partners, partner." I stuck out my hand, determined to try to make the best of things.

Michael stared at my outstretched hand as if he thought I may have recently sneezed into it, but after a moment, he reached out and grasped it with his own in a firm, warm grip.

"Partners," he said, pumping my hand up and down twice before dropping it.

I noticed that he hovered his hand over his pant leg for a second, as if he wanted to wipe his palm. He saw me looking and shot me a weak smile.

"I have to get back to work," he said. He left the booth and headed towards the exit.

"Wait, we need a name! What are we making? Where do I find you?" I called out to his retreating back.

I leaned my elbows on the countertop and cradled my head in my hands. *Oh good grief, what have I gotten myself into?*

Chapter 3

As I drove out of the parking lot, I tried to reassure myself that this was not going to turn out to be an unmitigated disaster. Twenty-five thousand dollars would still pay off my student loans and leave enough seed money to start a (very) small business.

Mr. Michael Brandon may be a top contender for the world's biggest jerk, but I only had to tolerate him for about a week, then after the holidays were over, I would be leaving Pinewood Corners—either to embark on my new life, or to return to my old one. Either way, my future wouldn't include Michael Brandon.

Driving slowly down Main Street amidst the holiday glitz, I once again noticed the new coffee shop. Glancing at the dashboard clock, I saw that I still had plenty of time before Grandma Jo expected me for dinner, so I impulsively pulled into one of the slanted parking spots in front of the coffee shop that was marked with a sign that read "Java Hut Parking Only."

Something jogged my memory, and I recalled that Grandma Jo had mentioned something about Mayor Reese investing in the opening of a new coffee shop, so this must be the place. I grabbed my purse off the seat next to me and jumped out of the Jeep.

"Mikki? Mikki Branson, is that you?" a throaty voice called out.

I turned and saw a stunning woman, slim and tall, with long gleaming black hair flowing from under a velvety cream knit hat, down over the shoulders of a red wool designer coat. She reached up to remove her fancy sunglasses, and I recognized Rayna Reese, my high school nemesis. My stomach dropped, and I reminded myself that high school was a long time ago and that we were both adults now.

I smiled. "Rayna, hi, you look great! How's it going?"

Rayna smiled back, her perfect white teeth gleaming in the afternoon sunlight. "Oh, thank you, dear, things are going fabulously," she said, looking me up and down.

I was suddenly very conscious of my old non-designer skinny jeans (*were skinny jeans out?*), scuffed brown boots and worn thrift store imitation down jacket.

"I heard you were in town," Rayna continued, "I assume you're visiting your darling old Grandmother, Joanna." Rayna flipped her shining hair over her shoulder.

"Yes," I replied, trying to sound as cool and casual as Rayna had. "I'm also here to enter the bake off."

Rayna's eyes narrowed. "How nice," she said. "My father thinks the bake off will be very good financially for the town. I was one of the first confirmed contestants, of course."

"Of course," I murmured, already feeling anxious to escape the conversation.

"So, anyone new in your life, or still just your cat?"

"What? How do you know I have a cat?"

"Oh, you know, social media and all that," Rayna replied vaguely with a wave of one perfectly manicured hand. "I'm just getting out of a serious relationship with an up-and-coming politician. He wanted a trophy wife, and I'm just not ready to give up my career."

Rayna ran the small weekly local paper, which her father also happened to own, which was the main reason that the *Pinewood Courier* was rather more like the *National Enquirer* in tone than a legitimate journalistic paper.

"I see," I replied noncommittally. "It was nice running into you and catching up, Rayna, but I really have to get going." I moved to walk past her and into the coffee shop.

Just then, a man approached. He was wearing a beautiful camel hair coat and a Burberry patterned scarf that looked like cashmere. He strolled up to Rayna and planted a kiss on her cheek. "Hello, darling," he said.

"Hi, Daddy," she replied, "You remember Mikki Branson, Joanna Morton's granddaughter." She looked in my direction.

"Of course. How is your grandmother doing?" he asked, extending his gloved hand to me. I shook it, the smell of fine leather tickling my nostrils.

"Hi, Mayor Reese. Grandma Jo is doing great, thanks. Nice to see you." I pumped his hand briefly and let it go. "I was about to go in and try some coffee at the new coffeehouse," I said.

"Wonderful, I hope you like it. I felt that it was time the town had a gourmet option for their daily cuppa," the mayor said, beaming at me. "I'm glad we got the place up and running in time for the festival and the bake off." He squeezed his daughter's shoulders affectionately. "My Rayna here is entered in the contest and I know she'll make me proud."

Rayna smiled up at him, showing off her perfect teeth. *Probably veneers,* I thought cattily.

"Yes, she told me just now. I'm giving the contest a shot myself."

"Really?" Mayor Reese asked, raising his brows. His hair was perfectly white at the temples, as if Hollywood makeup artists had sprayed them to make him look like a stereotypical mayor. I tried to smile, and an awkward silence descended.

"Well, it was great seeing you both. I'd better run if I want to grab a coffee. I told my grandma that I'd be home in time for dinner."

"Tell your lovely grandmother hello," the mayor said.

"Sure thing, Mayor Reese. Bye, Rayna. Maybe we'll run into each other again."

"Yes, we must talk again soon. Ta ta!" She popped her sunglasses back on and turned to go as I pulled open the door of the coffee shop.

A merry jingle from a string of bells hanging from the handle accompanied me through the door as I stepped into the warm and gloriously coffee-scented air. Soft jazzy holiday music floated from speakers mounted in the high ceiling. The warm, diffused lighting gently reflected off the olive-green walls decorated with stylized prints of coffee cups. Various tables with high-backed chairs and cozy booths enticed me to sit and stay a while.

I spotted a counter in the back with ordering and pick up areas on either side of a glass case that contained various baked treats that paired well with a cup of coffee. Patrons sat at the tables and in the booths, conversing in low tones or staring at phones or laptops. A large artificial tree strung with twinkling white lights and little coffee cup ornaments dominated one corner.

I approached the counter, my attention focused on the menu board above the back of the counter wall. The door to what I assumed was a back room or kitchen swung open and I turned to smile at the barista. My smile froze as I recognized none other than Michael "The Jerk" Brandon. My new baking partner.

"What are you doing here?" I demanded.

"Clearly, I work here," he said flatly. "What are you doing here?"

"It may seem weird, but I saw the coffee cup on the sign and thought I might be able to order some coffee in here," I retorted. "It's a good thing I stopped in, too, after your disappearing act in the tent. We need to come up with a game plan for the bake off."

Michael opened his mouth to speak, but I continued, "I don't like this situation, and you probably like it even less, judging from how you wanted to wipe away my cooties after we shook hands, but we're stuck together in this, and I'm in this contest for the win, so you'd better suck it up, buttercup."

Michael compressed his finely sculpted lips together until they almost disappeared. He took in a very deep, long breath, released it, muttered "nine, ten" under his breath, and with exaggerated patience, he said, "I did not 'disappear.' I had to get back to work, as I told you. This town is so small, I figured that I would easily find you. I know that your grandmother is Joanna Morton, and she lives out on Sugarplum Lane."

At my look of sputtering outrage, he said, "Relax, I'm not a stalker. Mrs. Morton is a regular customer here. She picks up a bag of beans every Tuesday. How about a caramel latte?"

He didn't wait for my reply, just busied himself behind the counter, grinding beans, tamping them into the machine, steaming the milk, adding caramel syrup, and mixing a latte in a light olive-green ceramic mug that he placed on the counter in front of me.

There was no way he could have known that caramel lattes were my favorite drink to order at a coffeehouse … unless Grandma Jo had told him?

"Thanks," I said, pulling out my wallet. I half expected him to comp the drink after he had been so rude to me, but he just stood there waiting for me to produce my debit card.

I paid for the drink and took a sip. It was delicious, the sweet caramel and creamy milk rounding out the dark bitter edge of the espresso. Everything was smooth and perfectly balanced.

"This is really good," I said grudgingly. He pressed his lips together as the bells on the door announced the arrival of another customer. I took my cup and wandered over to one of the open tables and sat down.

After Michael took care of the customer, who just wanted a muffin, he came out from behind the counter and approached my table. Wiping his hands on his apron, he sat down across from me.

"So," I said, looking up from my phone, "the great man condescends to sit with the likes of me."

To my surprise, he reached out and grabbed my phone and started typing away.

"What do you think you're doing?" I demanded.

"I'm typing a text to myself so we'll have one another's numbers," he said, glancing up at me. "You realize that you don't know anything about me." I heard a text alert ding from his pocket and he placed my phone on the table in front of me.

"And you don't know anything about me, yet you decided from the get-go that I was out to get you, or sabotage you, or something. You decided that I was too low-class to even shake my hand. You're right, I don't know anything about you, but I do know that we need to work together and come up with something that will knock the judges' socks off. I meant it when I told you that I was in this to win. I have a lot riding on this bake off." I snatched my phone from the table.

"I happen to agree with you," Michael said coolly. "I'm not thrilled to split the winnings, but half is better than none, and there doesn't seem to be any other way around this mess than figuring out how we can work together. I don't intend to lose, and I need to know you're going to pull your weight and not flake out on me."

"You've got a real way with words, you know that?" I said. "I'll have you know that I am fully trained—" Just then the bells on the door rang again. Michael started to rise from his seat.

"Wait," I said, "We need to talk and plan, uninterrupted. When are you off shift?"

"Eight," he replied, "but I'm, uh, busy." Michael hustled off to deal with the group of new customers.

How could Michael insist in one breath that he had no intention of losing this competition but then tell me in the next breath that he was too "busy" to meet up to plan and strategize as soon as possible? I polished off my latte, rose, and approached the counter.

Michael was busy whipping up drinks for the trio of new customers—three high-school aged girls by the look of them. I placed a five-dollar bill in the tip jar, making eye contact with Michael.

"I guess you know where to find me when you can manage to carve out the time. We need a team name by tomorrow." With that, I stalked out of the shop, trailed by a chorus of giggles from the girls.

*   *   *

I pulled the Jeep into the carport and parked next to my dusty old Chevy. The skies were cloudy in the frozen dusk as evening set in. Grandma Jo might be right about her weather prediction. The air was soft and carried the scent of snow and the temperature was dropping rapidly. My breath left little clouds in the air as I made my way to the house under the glow of the Christmas lights as they winked on.

"Grandma, I'm back!" I called out as I entered through the side door. Napoleon snuffled and wagged as I patted him. Acorn was still perched warily on the back of the couch.

I sat down on the little blue padded bench next to the door to yank my boots off. I grabbed my fuzzy slippers that had thoughtfully been placed under the bench by my Grandma and went off in search of her.

"Grandma Jo?" I called, wandering further into the little house, accompanied by Napoleon. The air was redolent with the savory scent of our impending dinner. It smelled like a roast or maybe stew, deep and rich and beefy, tinged with herbs.

"I'm in my studio!" Grandma's voice drifted down the hall.

I went towards the back of the house, where Grandma had enclosed half the back porch to create her studio, where she made beautiful custom quilts that sold for eye-popping amounts of money in her Etsy shop. Grandma had always made the finest quilts in the county, and I was glad that she had found a way to earn money doing something that she loved. That was all anyone could ask from a career, really.

"What are you working on now?" I asked, leaning against the doorframe.

"A bride's quilt," she replied without looking up from the quilting hoop on its stand as she stitched. "The bridal party is chipping in to surprise her. The wedding is on Valentine's Day."

I knew that quilts took a long time to complete, and a bride's quilt, with each square representing a different theme of love and marriage, would take an especially long time to finish. I wandered over to the quilt frame in the corner of the room to inspect what she had already completed.

The embroidery and workmanship were exquisite. One square showcased two gold bands intertwined inside a heart with golden wings. Another showed joined hands with a glorious sunset behind them, and a third depicted wedding bells in a church belfry. The center square displayed the name of the bride and groom, along with the date of the wedding, surrounded by hearts and flowers.

"This is gorgeous," I said, leaning over to examine the squares. I knew better than to reach out and touch anything.

"Thank you, dear. I'm just about at a good stopping point here." She pulled the needle through a scrap of fabric that composed a tiny petal on a rose in a bouquet. "Just have to sew the ribbon onto the bouquet now," she muttered, knotting off the thread.

She took off the magnifying lenses that she wore over her normal glasses, then took off the glasses as well and rubbed her eyes. "How about a nice pot of tea before dinner?" she asked, sliding her glasses back on. The purple frames paired well with her rosy complexion and silver hair.

"Sure, Grandma, that sounds good," I said, turning to head to the kitchen. Grandma Jo clicked off her work lamp and followed me down the hall.

My grandmother's kitchen was home to me, more than any place else in the world. The walls were a warm yellow, and the blond wood cabinets and the blue willow pattern china plates on the walls along with the copper pots hanging above the butcher block island created a cozy and relaxing atmosphere.

Grandma busied herself putting on the kettle at the big gas stove where the blue enameled cast-iron dutch oven bubbled away. I went to the cabinet to the right of the sink and grabbed two thick, white ceramic mugs. "You may be right, it does feel like snow," I told her, setting the mugs onto the island.

"I know I'm right, my hip always acts up when it's going to snow," she replied as she dropped several tea bags into the Spode Christmas tree teapot that she'd had ever since I could remember.

"Did you get all checked in?" she asked as she sank down onto one of the blue and yellow toile patterned cushioned stools that surrounded the kitchen island.

"Sort of," I replied. "I guess another guy signed up that has a name that's so close to mine, they thought we were the same person with a duplicate entry. We had to agree to sign up as a team so we could both still compete."

"Why, that's outrageous," Grandma Jo said. "How can they expect you to team up with somebody you've never even met?"

I shrugged. "They would've refunded my entry fee, but I didn't want to drop out, and neither did he. I don't think we have a choice."

"Well, things tend to work out the way that they're meant to. What are you fixing to make together?"

"That's just it. I have no idea," I said. "He had to leave right away to go back to work at the coffee shop, and he said he's busy after he's off shift. Busy!" I huffed and got up to retrieve the shrieking kettle.

"Wait a second, you said he works at the coffee shop? Is his name Michael? Blond fellow, handsome?"

"He mentioned that you stopped in to buy coffee beans," I said, skirting around the "handsome" comment.

"Oh, yes, the beans from Java Hut are the best!" Grandma beamed. "That Michael is so nice and polite," she said.

"Well, that certainly wasn't my experience with him," I told her. I poured the boiling water into the teapot and gently secured the lid.

Grandma Jo sighed. "I'm sure sorry if he gave you a rough time. His mama is sick, she's in the hospital. Some sort of degenerative thing, I don't know the details. Michael is really private about it."

I felt a little ashamed. "I'm afraid I gave Michael a bit of a rough time myself," I said. "I didn't know about his mother."

"That's why he's in town," Grandma Jo said. "His mama moved here a few years back, after Michael's daddy died. Michael was off at some sort of fancy law school or internship or some such thing, and his mama took ill, so he dropped everything to come here and move into her house and help take care of her."

She expertly poured the tea into the two mugs without spilling a drop and pushed one towards me. Picking up the other mug and cupping her hands around it, she blew on the surface of the liquid and sipped. Closing her eyes, she sighed. "Nothing like a good cup of tea on a cold winter's night."

"I can see why he was so determined to stay in the contest," I said. "I'm sure that the prize money from the bake off would go a long way towards helping out his mother." I picked up my cup and sipped. Peppermint flooded my senses, refreshing and cool.

"Well, he does bake all the treats in the coffee shop," Grandma Jo said. "That's why Mayor Reese was so excited to hire him to run the place. He has baking skills as well as barista experience."

"What? I had no idea," I said, flashing back to Michael telling me that I knew nothing about him. That was certainly an understatement.

"Why would you know that, unless he told you?" My Grandma patted my hand. "Don't be so hard on yourself. You're a clever and talented girl, you'll work it all out." She looked at the clock over the stove. "Goodness, the stew will be done soon. I'd better get the rolls in the oven."

I reached out and grabbed her arm. "Grandma, how about we skip the rolls this time?"

Chapter 4

The next morning, I was in the kitchen making coffee—or rather, attempting to make coffee. Grandma's high-end machine was complicated enough with the assistance of a caffeine boost. In my sleep-fuzzed state, it was nearly impossible to figure out. Acorn watched the proceedings, tail twitching with feline amusement, from his perch on the island.

"Oh, shoot!" I stomped my foot in frustration as the machine beeped at me. Grandma Jo came into the room, fully dressed for the day in sassy red slacks and a green sweatshirt adorned with a pattern of tiny red elf hats. I turned to her. "Please make this work," I pleaded, wringing my hands.

"Mikki," she scolded, sounding scandalized, "why aren't you dressed yet? It's nearly half past seven."

I glanced down at my black thermal pajama ensemble. "Because I haven't had my coffee yet," I replied with a jaw-cracking yawn.

"I'll get the coffee started and make us some bacon and eggs. You go on and get yourself pretty for the day." She shooed me out and turned to the coffee machine.

"You'll have to settle for presentable," I muttered as I shuffled out of the kitchen.

I was heading for my room when I was startled by the chiming of the doorbell. As the opening notes of "We Wish You a Merry Christmas" rang out from the customized door chime, the caller also began pounding on the door. I stomped over to the door and flung it open.

Michael Brandon stood on the doorstep, wearing a dark leather bomber jacket, jeans, chunky boots and a blue and gray plaid scarf. The bright morning sunlight backlit his blond hair like a halo. His hand was raised to knock again.

"What," I snarled, "are you doing here at this hour?"

He lowered his hand. "I thought we could get started with our bake off planning this morning before I have to be on shift at the Java Hut, but I see that you're not a morning person." His breath puffed out in little clouds on the frigid morning air. He put his hands in his pockets and rocked back onto his heels.

I really wanted to read him the riot act for having the nerve to come knocking so early in the morning, but I thought about the bake off officiant telling us that we needed a team name by the end of the day today.

"I suppose so, but I would've appreciated a call first," I said. I saw the corners of his mouth twitching as he looked me up and down.

I glanced at the hall mirror near the door. My fine brown hair was standing up in a frizzly bush at the crown of my head and my pajama pants were sagging comically low. I was about to make a defensive comment when I heard footsteps behind me.

"Oh, Michael, good morning! How's your mama?" Grandma Jo stepped up beside me, smiling cheerfully.

"Good morning, Mrs. Morton. She's holding steady, thank you."

"Oh, that's good to hear," Grandma Jo said warmly. She turned to me. "Mikki, why on earth are you standing here in your pajamas? And why haven't you invited this nice young man in yet?"

"I was on my way to change when the doorbell rang," I explained.

"Well, Michael, I insist that you come in and join me for a cup of coffee. You can keep me company while Mikki gets dressed." She gave me a pointed look and, taking the hint, I headed for my room with a sigh as I heard Grandma Jo asking Michael if he had eaten breakfast yet.

*   *   *

When I returned to the kitchen a short time later, wearing my trusty jeans and a heather-gray turtleneck sweater with my hair tamed into a braid down my back, my grandma was at the stove piling fluffy yellow scrambled eggs onto a platter from her old cast-iron pan. A plate of crisp and fragrant strips of bacon was already waiting on a platter on the island where Michael sat, sipping from a mug.

"Just in time," Grandma Jo said, smiling at me. "Why don't you set the table and take the food over while I pour more coffee."

I set about my tasks while Michael watched me.

"Need any help?" he asked.

I shook my head, my favorite big silver hoops swinging from my ears. "Nope, I've got it, thanks." I put out plates and forks efficiently on the round table set in the space by the kitchen's bay window that overlooked the bird feeder in the backyard.

Grandma Jo came over with the coffee cups and set them down. "Everyone please have a seat," she said.

We all settled in and passed platters of bacon and eggs around. For a few moments, there was no talking as we tucked into plates full of food.

"This is excellent, Mrs. Morton," Michael said.

"Thank you. I always say that a hearty breakfast leads to a productive day," Grandma Jo replied.

"What's on your agenda today, Gran?" I asked her.

"I need to run down to the Java Hut for my weekly beans, and then stop by the grocery store and then I'll spend some time working on the bride's quilt. I also hope to find time to run down to Higgins' tree lot and pick out a tree to decorate."

"Oh, that reminds me—" Michael plucked his jacket from the back of his chair and dug around inside the recesses of the pockets until he produced a small black bag. He held the bag out to Grandma Jo. "Espresso roast, right?"

"Thank you! What do I owe you?" Grandma Jo reached out to take the bag of coffee beans.

Michael waved her off. "Not a thing. Buy ten bags of beans, get the eleventh free." He winked.

"Well, that's one errand I can cross off my list," Grandma said with delight.

"Is that what we're drinking now?" I asked. "It's very good."

"Yes, I told you that the beans from Java Hut were the best," Grandma Jo said, taking another sip from her cup and closing her eyes rapturously.

"So," Michael said, wiping his hands on a napkin, "I stopped by the tent this morning on my way over here and submitted our team name."

I dropped my fork onto my plate with a clatter. "What?" I asked, outrage building within me. "What team name? We haven't even discussed that."

Michael looked taken aback. "We're under a time crunch. I thought I'd get a minor and unimportant detail out of the way."

Innocently unaware of the undercurrent of tension, Grandma Jo asked, "What name did you choose, Michael?"

"MB Squared," he told her, looking unnervingly proud of himself.

"How clever!" Grandma Jo enthused. "Because you both have the same initials."

I gritted my teeth. "I would have appreciated it if you had bothered to run something as significant as our team name by me first," I said. "The word 'team' implies that we are in collaboration with one another."

Michael shrugged. "I didn't think it was that big of a deal. The recipe is what's going to win the contest, not our name."

"I suppose you've already got that underway as well?" I asked him, sarcasm twisting my voice.

"Well sure," he replied, "You can assist me in making the recipe that originally I intended to make, my mother's recipe for walnut kolacky."

"I'm sorry, what? Kolacky? *Assistant!?*"

"Kolacky is a traditional Hungarian cookie with a cream cheese dough wrapped around a walnut filling," Michael said patiently, ignoring my outrage.

"I *know* what kolacky is," I said. "I made them in culinary school."

His blue eyes widened with surprise. "Culinary school?" he asked.

"With a focus on pastry," I snapped as I rose and began clearing the table.

"Great," Michael said, "then you'll be a perfect assistant."

I slammed the plates into the sink.

"Mikki, please be careful with the dishes," Grandma Jo admonished me. "Why don't I take care of that while you young folks go on into the parlor and talk."

"Sorry, Grandma, thanks," I said. I stalked towards the front room without looking at Michael. I heard his chair scrape the floor tiles as he rose, presumably to follow me.

I sat in the wing-back chair, leaving the couch for Michael. He sat smack in the middle of the sofa, arms crossed.

"You have a lot of nerve, showing up here at the crack of dawn to tell me that you've made all the decisions for our team," I began.

"I explained to you that time was of the essence, and I saw no point in wasting any time debating something as silly as our team name, or arguing about what to make. If we move forward with my original choice, we can get started with some practice batches right away and have the recipe perfected by next Friday."

"Did it ever occur to you that perhaps I had intended to use a recipe of my own?" I was so furious that my hands twisting in my lap were turning white.

"Sure," he shrugged and said, "but my recipe is proven. My mom has won several bake offs with that recipe. None of this scale, of course, but …" he trailed off as I glared at him.

"Mr. Michael Brandon, I have never met anyone so arrogant and bossy, and since you won't ask me, I'll tell you. I intended to enter the bake off with my Grandma Jo's recipe for cardamom sugar cookies."

Michael waved the idea away. "Too simple," he said. "We have to really stand out to the judges. We can't win just on your good looks."

"Simple!?" I sputtered, "But you've never even tried them. They melt in your mouth, they're DELICIOUS!" *Wait, did he just say I was good looking? Focus, Mikki!*

"Oh, I'm sure they're fine for a ladies' tea party or luncheon," Michael said condescendingly, "but not of the caliber that we need to win this contest."

He rose and shrugged his jacket on. "We'll go with the kolacky. I'll meet you back here this evening at seven, after I'm off work. I'll bring the ingredients and we can do a test batch tonight." He knotted his scarf at his neck, tipped his head, and strode to the front door.

I sat in stunned silence, feeling as if I had just been run over by a snow plow as the door shut firmly behind Michael. I dropped my head back against the chair and pressed my palms to my eyes. Honestly, what *had* I gotten myself into?

Chapter 5

We piled into Grandma Jo's Jeep. As I strapped on my seatbelt, I noticed a pile of colorful nylon fabric puddled on the ground in front of the house, peeking through the dusting of newly fallen snow.

"Did you get a new blow-up for the yard?" I asked.

"Yep. Santa in his sleigh, pulled by Rudolph. I wanted the one that featured all eight reindeer, but my front yard isn't big enough," Grandma replied.

She put the Jeep in reverse and we backed out of the driveway. As the SUV made its way through the neighborhood, Grandma Jo honked and waved at various neighbors who were out shoveling walkways, sweeping porches, and walking dogs.

I stared out the window at the light coating of snow that had fallen in the night. The sun shone on the white blanket covering the ground, illuminating the sparkling crystals. I squinted, wishing I had thought to grab my sunglasses.

Main Street was even more festive than the previous day, boasting garlands of holly leaves accented with vivid red berries winding around the lampposts. The merchants had begun setting out the red and green jars filled with flickering battery-operated candles to line the sidewalks and illuminate them at night.

The charming luminarias were a beloved Pinewood Corners holiday tradition. Back in the day, they had been traditional paper sacks with tealight candles nestled in a layer of sand, but in modern days, the fire marshal had put the kibosh on open flames inside paper bags. I personally thought that the colorful glass jars were prettier, sparkling rubies and emeralds paving the streets like the yellow brick road leading to Oz.

"What are you planning to do with your afternoon?" Grandma Jo asked, startling me out of my reverie. "I hope you still have time for tree shopping."

"Oh, well, Michael said he's coming over this evening to bake. In the meantime, I thought I might look up Lacey around lunchtime, see how she's doing," I said, referring to my high school bestie, Lacey Franklin. She was Lacey Crawford now, having been married to Jed Crawford. Lacey and Jed got married right after high school graduation, but the marriage had fizzled out a couple of years ago. Jed had inherited the hardware store after his father retired, and he and Lacey shared custody of their daughter, Claire.

"I'm so glad you two have kept in touch. Lacey is such a sweetheart. Since she took over as head librarian, she's instituted so many new reading programs and events. It's really brought traffic back to the library."

I knew Grandma Jo had a secret predilection for bodice-ripper romances, especially if they involved swashbuckling pirates and saucy heroines.

"Yeah, we tag each other on social media and manage a few texts here and there," I said. "We're both pretty busy."

"You should never be too busy for a true friend," Grandma Jo said. "In the end, people matter, and relationships matter. Nobody is coming around with a productivity checklist when your time's up."

I chuckled to myself at the image of the Grim Reaper holding a pad and pen instead of a scythe. I knew she was right, though, and I resolved to stop by the library once we got the groceries home and stashed away.

Grandma flicked on the turn signal and pulled into the parking lot of the Fresh Stop, Pinewood Corners' main grocery store. I grabbed a shopping cart as Grandma Jo fussed around with her purse and pockets, organizing her list and coupons.

"Grandma, you should use digital coupons," I told her.

"I do," she said, "and I also use paper coupons if I have them. Why throw away money?"

She was always thrifty, and she knew how to stretch a budget. I was grateful to have learned that from her. We passed through the automatic doors into the warmth of the store. Almost immediately, we were greeted by a loud "Hey, Jo!"

Grandma turned her head and a big smile stretched across her face as she saw Sheriff Weaver striding over. She blushed as he took off his hat and gave her a little wink.

"I see you ladies are having a nice visit so far. Running some errands today?"

"Yes, we're just stocking up on some supplies for the week," Grandma said. She fidgeted with her coat buttons and shuffled her feet.

"By the way, that cherry cobbler was some of the best I've ever had, Jo."

Grandma Jo dipped her head modestly. "Oh, I just threw it together. It's an easy recipe to make."

"Well, it was wonderful," the sheriff said. "I still have your dish. Maybe, if you're going to be home this evening, I could stop by and return it."

"I suppose that would be fine. I'm planning on spending the evening decorating my tree."

Sheriff Weaver grinned. "I hear Higgins has some fine trees this year. Do you need any help hauling one home?"

Grandma Jo blushed again. "Oh, no, I'm sure we'll manage, thank you. I've got Mikki to help me."

"Well then, I'll see you ladies later. Happy shopping!" He put his hat back on and pulled on the brim in a salute as he sauntered away.

"Grandma Jo!" I teased. "You were blushing like a schoolgirl!"

"Oh, cut it out, it's nothing." She waved me off. "He's a very nice man."

"Nice and hot, a real silver fox," I joked.

She tossed her head and sniffed, refusing to take the bait. "Now, the first thing I need is some oranges. I'm going to make pomanders with the extra cloves after I make my pumpkin pies." She stalked away, clutching her list.

I laughed as I steered the cart towards the produce department.

*   *   *

The air was cold and clear as we made our way out to the parking lot towards the Jeep with our cart full of goodies. I had decided to pick up the ingredients for Grandma Jo's cardamom sugar cookies, regardless of what Mr. High-and-Mighty thought he was dictating. Grandma hit the button on her key to unlock the Jeep and pop the back hatch. As I began to unload the bags from the cart, a voice from behind startled me.

"Mikki? How's it going?"

I jumped and lost my hold on the bag I was loading into the trunk. Oranges rolled in every direction.

I turned and saw a tall, stout man with dark hair and warm brown eyes smiling at me. He was wearing a law officer's uniform, like Sheriff Weaver's. His name tag read "Deputy Willis."

I broke out into a grin. "Tom! Oh my goodness, it's been a long while. I'm good, thank you. How are you?"

Tom's smile widened. He started gathering up the wayward oranges. "Let me help you with these," he said. "I'm doing well. I just got hired full time as deputy sheriff this year.

I'm so happy that I came back to Pinewood Corners. After college, I realized that this is where my heart is."

He tossed the last of the oranges into their bag and placed them in the SUV. "How about you, Mikki? Are you just here for a visit with your grandma, or are you back permanently, too?" His brown eyes twinkled as he turned to Grandma Jo. "And hello to you, too, Ms. Morton. You're looking lovely, as always."

Grandma Jo laughed and swatted his arm. "Oh, Tom, you're such a flatterer." She shot a significant look at me and jumped into the driver's seat, leaving me standing alone with Tom. He shut the back door and turned to me.

I licked my lips nervously. I was remembering all the times with him in the past, hanging out, talking, holding hands. A few short, sweet kisses and honeyed words and promises to keep in touch that we had meant to keep, but failed. "I'm just visiting. I'm here to see Grandma Jo, of course, but also to enter the bake off."

"Oh, yeah," Tom replied, snapping his fingers. "I remember your grandma telling me that you had put yourself through culinary school. She said you were working at some sort of high-end resort, a really great career."

"It's just a regular old resort," I said, embarrassed that Grandma Jo was at it again with her tendency to exaggerate. "Nothing to brag about."

"Still, if you love what you do, you never work a day in your life. Isn't that what they say?" Tom looked at me hopefully. It was obvious that he enjoyed his work immensely.

"I suppose they do say that," I replied with a shrug. No need to go into the details of my life of drudgery baking rolls.

Tom fiddled with his hat, spinning the brim in his hands. He cleared his throat. "If you're not busy tomorrow afternoon, the ice rink is opening tomorrow. I thought maybe you'd like to go ice skating. You know, for old time's sake."

I was hit with a flash of memory, the two of us clutching one another's hands as we wobbled more or less around the ice rink, snowflakes settling in his long eyelashes as he threw back his head and laughed at my lack of balance. I used to blame my stumbling on all the twinkling lights blinding me. We did have fun back then.

I suddenly longed for a few hours of that joyful and carefree feeling. I had so much to do to prepare for the bake off, but I deserved a little amusement, too.

On impulse, I took the plunge. "Sure, that sounds great. I warn you, though, my balance isn't any better now than it was back then!"

"Oh, I think I can support you just fine," Tom replied, sounding pleased. "Should I pick you up at your grandma's?"

"I'll meet you there. I'm not sure what all is on my agenda for tomorrow yet."

"Okay then, I'll meet you by the entrance to the rink at three tomorrow!" Tom placed his hat on his head and beamed a wide smile at me.

"See you then!" I waved as he headed towards the Ford Explorer marked with the Wingate County law enforcement logo parked a few spaces away. As I climbed into the Jeep, I realized that I hadn't allowed myself to feel supported for a very long time.

Chapter 6

I parked my Chevy in one of the last open parking spots in the lot adjacent to the town library. The place looked packed. As the automatic doors slid open, the unmistakable whiff of paper and binding and books wafted over me like a comforting hug. Libraries all smelled the same.

I glanced around and saw a group of children sitting on the floor in the corner of a brightly lit and colorful area hemmed in by short bookshelves painted in primary colors. The children were all staring raptly at the petite redhead who sat in a chair holding up an oversized, thin book.

"And it was still hot." The redhead closed the book and the children all clapped and cheered. The redhead looked up and caught sight of me and grinned. She excused herself from the children and made her way over to me.

"*Where the Wild Things Are*, eh?"

"You know it. It's a classic for a reason." Lacey threw her arms around me and gave me a squeeze. "Why didn't you text me that you were coming home?"

"I was taking care of a lot of things," I replied, stepping back. "I entered the bake off."

"Oh goody," Lacey said, rubbing her hands together. "Someone needs to beat the pants off of Rayna for once."

I laughed. "Thanks for the vote of confidence. Do you get a lunch hour?"

"Since I'm on a librarian's salary, I usually brown bag it. But I think I can spare half a sandwich, if you'd care to join me in my office." She beckoned me to follow as she headed towards the rear of the building.

"How are Jed and the hardware store doing?" I followed behind Lacey as we wove through rows of bookshelves to a door marked "Head Librarian."

She shrugged. "Jed's fine. Last I heard, the store is doing okay, but it's tough to compete with Walmart, and they opened a Home Depot in Springrock last year. Have a seat."

The office was small but cute and cozy, with posters of classic book covers on the walls and plants on the windowsill. I took a seat in the lone guest chair as Lacey settled behind the desk. She produced a sandwich baggie from a purple insulated lunch bag and offered me half the sandwich.

"Turkey and Swiss on sourdough, mustard and mayo with tomato and lettuce."

"Thanks," I said, grabbing the sandwich. Lacey dug around in a drawer and pulled out a handful of napkins and put them in the middle of the desk. I snagged one and placed my sandwich half on it.

Lacey poured hot tea from a tall Thermos into two disposable cups. "You'll have to come for dinner if you have time before you leave town. Claire would be over the moon to see you. She's grown so much since you last saw her."

"I'll bet. She's almost four now, right?"

We continued chatting and catching up as we ate, relaxing into the easy rhythm of old friends. I told her about my unfulfilled career dreams and hopes for the future, and she told me how happy she was with the progress she had made with the library and shared her struggles as a single parent. She and Jed were on good terms, but it was still difficult for her to balance her career and parenting her daughter.

"I ran into Tom Willis this morning at the Fresh Stop."

"Whoa, are you guys rekindling your romance?" Lacey wiggled her eyebrows and held out a baggie filled with potato chips.

"I don't know. I doubt it. Tom seems content to live in Pinewood Corners, and I don't think I'm ready to settle down and be a cop's wife just yet." I pulled a handful of chips out of the baggie. "I left town to chase my dreams of building my culinary career, and I still want to pursue them." I crunched into a salty chip with satisfaction.

"I'm not asking you if you're going to marry him next weekend," Lacey said. "I'm just asking if you're going to spend a little extracurricular time with him. He's grown into a very handsome man." She winked at me. "You know that Rayna has had her eye on him for the past few months."

"That surprises me, I thought an officer of the law was too low on the social ladder for her. I did agree to meet up with him to go ice skating tomorrow."

"That sounds like fun. Maybe I should bring Claire out for an afternoon of skating and mulled cider and cocoa. It's technically Jed's week to have Claire, but I'm sure he won't mind. He hired his nephew, Jerry, as assistant manager at the hardware store last year. It's been nice for him to have a backup person to help run the store. It frees up Jed for more time with Claire now that we share custody."

"Great, maybe I'll see you guys there."

"What are you making for the bake off?" Lacey asked, dabbing her mouth with a napkin.

"That's a bit of a sore subject as of right now," I replied.

"Do tell!" Lacey leaned across the desk eagerly.

"Well, this guy, Michael Brandon, entered too, and I guess the contest people thought we were the same person because our names sound so alike, and now we're stuck sharing the last available booth."

"Michael Brandon? The barista at the coffee shop? He's even cuter than Tom!"

I rolled my eyes. "Sure, if you like the mean and pretty type. He's totally taking over and says we're making his mom's recipe for kolacky and he won't listen to anything I have to say."

Lacey leaned back in her chair and moaned. "If kolacky are those little diamond shaped pastry things with the nut filling that they have at the coffee shop sometimes, then you'll win for sure. Those things are *amazing*." She mimed wiping drool off her lips.

"Do you remember Grandma Jo's cardamom sugar cookies?" I asked. Her face lit up.

"I sure do! That's why I started hanging around with you, so I could come over after school and get my hands on those cookies." Her wide green eyes sparkled with mischief.

I laughed and my annoyance with her for praising the enemy evaporated.

A knock sounded on the office door. It opened and a harried-looking older woman in a green turtleneck and a Santa hat poked her head in.

"Sorry to interrupt, Ms. Crawford, but Mrs. Langtree is here to pick up the copy of that new Nicholas Sparks novel that she had on reserve, but we just can't find it anywhere."

Lacey smiled. "I'll be right there, Agnes." She turned to me. "Duty calls. It was wonderful seeing you. Let's get together again before you leave."

"Absolutely," I said, giving her a quick hug before we emerged from her office and went our separate ways.

*   *   *

My text tone dinged as I headed to my car, dodging the piles of slush that dotted the library's parking lot. It was a message from Grandma Jo.

Hey my girl, when you're done catching up with Lacey, meet me at Higgins' lot so we can get our tree. Let me know when you're on the way. Love, Grandma

I chuckled at the way she signed off. I had told her that I could always tell that it was her because she was in my contacts and her name came up on the text, but she persisted.

I typed back. *Hi Gran, I'm hopping in the car now, see you there.* I added a heart emoji and then, after a moment of hesitation, I added a Christmas tree emoji as well and hit the "send" button and got on the road.

The parking at Higgins' tree lot was full, which was just as well. The gravel was sparse and pitted and it was getting muddy by afternoon. I parked on the side street bordering the lot and looked around.

I spotted Grandma Jo talking to a tall, broad-shouldered man in a dark blue beanie and gray and blue plaid scarf. As I approached, my suspicions were confirmed. I was surprised that Michael was leaning against a 4-wheel drive pickup with a trailer hitch. He seemed to be a sports car guy to me.

"Hello, Grandma. Mr. Brandon." I made eye contact with each of them in turn, determined to be polite.

"Hi, Mikki," Grandma Jo said, "I'm so glad you were able to get here so quickly. I ran into Michael. He kindly offered to help me load up a tree, but I told him that I was meeting you here any moment." She smiled up at Michael as if he had offered to fund her retirement. I groaned inwardly, not wanting to offend my grandmother.

"What have you got there?" I asked, gesturing to the tiny tree that Michael held in one hand. "I see your holiday spirit is huge this year." I snickered.

"It's for my mom's room at the hospital," Michael said. "I hope it will add some cheer for her."

Embarrassed by my poor attempt at sarcasm, my cheeks flushed hotly. "Oh, that's so nice of you." I looked around and noticed a group of tables nearby with potted poinsettias in red, white, and pink. I reached over and grabbed a pink one. "Please allow me to buy this for you to take to her as well."

He looked flustered. "Oh, that's not necessary. She doesn't even know you." He waved the plant away.

"Suit yourself," I replied, replacing the pot on the table. "It was nice running into you. Grandma, ready to find the perfect tree?" I went to turn away from the ever-annoying Michael Brandon, but Grandma Jo foiled my plan.

"Michael, you seem to have a good eye. Why don't you help us find our tree?" She smiled up at him expectantly.

"Sure," he said, "how could I refuse?" He gestured with a bow. "Lead the way."

We wandered down the fragrant aisles created by the rows of trees, some towering over us and others no more than waist high. The air was crisp with the bracing scent of pine and the mood of the holidays washed over me, drowning me in nostalgic vibes.

I couldn't help but smile at the memories of Christmas mornings with my Grandma, and my parents, all of us singing carols around the tree with Mom always trying to drown out everybody else, exchanging gifts, drinking mulled cider and eggnog and cocoa, eating cookies and candies and savory roast dinners until we were all about to burst. My parents, forever the actors, always performed a scene from Dickens' *A Christmas Carol.*

Lost in the dreamland of Christmases past, I was startled out of my reverie by Grandma Jo's sudden shriek.

"There it is! That's the one!" She pointed to a six-foot Douglas fir with tight, full branches begging for ornaments and strands of lights.

A bearded man in jeans, heavy boots, and a brown canvas apron covering his puffy coat appeared. "Hey, Miz Morton. You settled on this one?" I recognized him vaguely from around town, he was a great-nephew to Mary Baumgartner, the principal of Pinewood High School, and he did lots of odd jobs and seasonal work around Pinewood Corners.

"Yes, Jared, thank you!" said Grandma.

He produced a pocket knife and cut the tree from the cable and pulled it out from the row. "You want me to help you to your car with this beauty?" Jared asked, pulling the ticket off the tree and handing it to my grandmother.

"No, no, that's quite all right. We have some muscle here already." She indicated Michael with a wave of her hand.

Jared leaned the tree towards Michael, who grabbed it with his gloved hand.

"Uh, thanks," Michael said as Jared strolled off towards another customer with a wave.

"Michael, why don't you take that over to my Jeep and start tying it to the roof while Mikki and I check out. And please let me pay for that, I insist." She indicated the miniature potted tree that sat on the ground next to Michael's feet.

He shuffled and hemmed and hawed about it, but my grandma can be a force to be reckoned with when she puts her foot down. A few minutes later, we were headed for the front tables carrying Michael's little tree.

Hank Higgins was manning the iPad at the front, and his hearty laugh greeted us. "Well, if it isn't the two most lovely ladies in Pinewood Corners!" he shouted jovially, waving us over. It was no coincidence that Hank Higgins bore a striking resemblance to jolly old Saint Nick himself, with his burgeoning belly and long white hair and beard and his twinkling blue eyes behind wire-framed glasses.

"That little guy gonna be your tree this year, Miz Morton?" he asked, raising his bushy white eyebrows.

"No, no," Grandma Jo reassured him, "I'm getting a lovely six foot Douglas fir for my place." She waved the tag from the tree at him. "This baby tree is for Michael Brandon, for his mama's room at the hospital."

Mr. Higgins was suddenly somber. "He's a good boy," he replied, as he entered the items into the iPad and gave us a total. Grandma Jo swiped her card, and we were on our way.

The parking lot was hectic, filled with other holiday shoppers and tree lot employees strapping trees to the roofs of various cars, vans, and SUVs. By the time we wound our way to Grandma Jo's Jeep, Michael was putting the finishing ties onto the Douglas fir, securing it to the vehicle's roof.

"Thank you, Michael," Grandma said. "That looks nice and solid. I think we'll make it home just fine." She handed him the little tree.

Michael accepted the tree, his face red. I wondered if it was from the frigid air or from embarrassment.

"Are you still planning on coming by to do some baking tonight?" I asked him.

"Of course," he replied, in a tone that implied that I might be either stupid or crazy. "We already agreed that we have to practice our recipe and perfect it in time for the contest."

"Yes, of course, *we* did," I mimicked his frigid tone as best I could.

He looked away, across the parking lot, not paying any attention to my reply. I glanced over to see what he was so fascinated by. A figure in a lavender coat and deep purple hat and scarf drifted towards us. *Rayna.*

"Why, Michael, hello, what are you doing here?" Rayna trilled through her nose in what I was sure she thought of as a musical voice. She extended both of her leather-gloved hands towards Michael as she approached.

I had no idea what she thought he was supposed to do— kiss them? Michael solved the problem by ignoring the gesture.

"I'm at the tree lot, so obviously I'm purchasing a tree." He held up the tiny tree. Well, at least he was blunt with every-one, not just me.

"How cute!" Rayna enthused. "Is it for Daddy's coffee shop?"

"No, it's for my mom's hospital room. I thought it might cheer her up."

"That's *so* sweet of you, Michael." She smiled and batted her thick eyelashes at him. Her eyes were an unusual deep violet, just like Elizabeth Taylor's, as she loved to mention to everyone.

She glanced around as if noticing Grandma Jo and me for the first time. "Hello, you two. Mind if I steal him away from you? I need some help getting my tree to my car. Higgins simply refuses to deliver, and I don't want my Lexus getting scratched."

I prayed for patience and the ability to hold my tongue. "He's not mine to give away, have at it," I replied, smiling sweetly as I saw a pained look cross Michael's face.

"Sure, Rayna, whatever you need," he said through gritted teeth as he shot me a glare. "I'll see you later, Michaela."

Rayna seized Michael's arm and thrust her hand into his elbow as she looked me up and down speculatively. She was probably dying to know why Michael would be seeing me later but had too much pride to ask. As they strolled away, I caught a few words in the crisp air—*poor thing … peaked years ago … so gentlemanly of you to offer your charity …*

With a low growl, I slung my purse over my shoulder. "Let's go, Grandma."

"See you at home, Mikki-girl," Grandma winked and climbed into her Jeep.

Chapter 7

"Ow!" I cried as the spiked needles of the tree branch thwacked me on the cheek.

"Sorry, honey, the twine slipped." Grandma Jo's voice was muffled as she struggled with her side of the tree. Together we managed to wrestle the gorgeous monstrosity into the stand and get it more or less balanced and secured.

"Now for the fun part, the decorating!" Grandma Jo waved her hand at the stacks of green plastic bins with red lids that I knew held her prized holiday tree ornaments, garlands, and strands of lights. Those bins had been around my entire life, their number only increasing over the years. There were a good dozen waiting to be opened.

"Grandma, surely all that won't fit on this tree," I protested.

"Nope, but we'll fish out the best ones, and the ones with the best memories," Grandma Jo replied.

"Why do you keep them all? Why not get rid of the ones that aren't 'the best ones'?" I asked her, genuinely curious.

"I'm saving them for you," she said as she struggled to pry the lid off of the nearest bin. "Your mama doesn't have any means to store them, living like a nomad, so that makes you my heir. One day, you'll have a home and family of your own and you'll want these decorations, mark my words."

I swallowed hard and blinked at her. My first impulse was to protest, to tell her that I had no use for these sentimental trappings and to refuse her offer. I was twenty-nine years old, and I had never had a serious relationship, other than with my career aspirations. I had no prospects on the horizon, and my grandmother's blithe assumptions of my future happy family only brought out fears that I had buried so deeply that I thought I had thrown away the key.

Deep down, I feared that I would always be alone and that after I lost my grandma to the inevitable, the holidays would forever after be a bleak reminder of all that I had lost and all that I had never found.

"Oh, well, thank you. I just don't have room in my little apartment for this stuff, so if you want to go ahead and get rid of it—"

"Nonsense," Grandma cut me off, her voice muffled as she leaned into the bin and burrowed around. "I know you don't need them now, but when you have your family home, you'll have plenty of room." She spoke with such conviction, I almost believed her.

"Oooh! Look at *this* one!" Grandma Jo extracted herself from the bin her head had been buried in and triumphantly held up a rumpled angel cut from a white paper plate, complete with a misshapen halo made from a yellow pipe cleaner and a face drawn on with crayon.

I rolled my eyes and sighed. "Grandma, why on earth do you still have that thing? I made that in first grade. It looks so, so—crude."

"Mikki!" she cried, sounding shocked. "This is one of my very favorite things to hang on the tree. It's very special, one that can never be replaced. I remember the day you gave it to me, and you were so proud of it." She beamed at the ornament again and carefully set it aside.

Just as she was leaning into the bin again, we were interrupted by a loud chorus of "Jingle Bells" from the door chime.

"Oh my, that must be Michael. You did say he was coming by tonight, didn't you?" Grandma Jo raised her voice over Napoleon's barking. Without waiting for an answer, she headed for the front door. She returned to the room a moment later, Michael in tow.

He was wearing his jeans, boots, leather bomber, and his blue hat and scarf combo. I pushed aside thoughts of how the hat and scarf brought out the blue in his eyes. I noticed that he was holding a bag from the Fresh Stop. Michael followed my gaze and held up the bag.

"I brought some ingredients for our baking session," he said. "And these are for you." Michael held out a gorgeous bouquet of flowers, red daisies and white carnations accented by baby's breath, with pine boughs artfully woven in. My heart skipped a beat, and then I realized that he was holding the flowers out to my grandma.

"Why, thank you, Michael. What a thoughtful gesture. And the flowers are absolutely lovely!" She graciously accepted the bouquet. "I'll just go and fetch a vase. These will really brighten up the kitchen table."

"Grandma, you might want to put those in a higher spot," I warned. "Acorn loves to eat flowers, and some varieties are poisonous to cats."

With a wink of acknowledgment, she carried the flowers into the kitchen. I could hear her rattling around, opening cabinets and running the sink. Michael and I stood awkwardly silent, alternating looking around the room and glancing briefly at each other.

"Here, let me put that in the kitchen," I said, reaching for the handles of the large canvas bag embossed with the red and white logo of the Fresh Stop. Michael pulled the bag in towards his body, stopping me.

"Nope," he said, "Nobody touches my ingredients, not even my assistant, until I measure them out."

My temper flared, heating my cheeks, and I remembered in an instant why this man irritated me so much.

"Assistant?" I cried. "I am a classically trained pastry chef. I am your teammate, equal in every way—no—*better*! I'm *better* than you in every way, and if you think for one minute—" I cut myself off in the midst of my tirade as I felt a delicate brush across my cheek. Puzzled, I looked at Michael. He was smiling as he held out his gloved hand.

"Glitter," he said, displaying his fingertips.

I must have still looked confused, because he elaborated. "You had some glitter on your cheek. Probably from all the decorating stuff." He waved his hand around to indicate the mountains of holiday totes scattered throughout the room. With a satisfied air, he strolled towards the kitchen, tote bag in hand.

Frustrated beyond words, I clutched my hands into fists and beat them against the rough fabric of the back of the easy chair next to me, my mouth open in a silent scream. This man was the most arrogant and condescending person I had ever met. He truly took the cake, pun definitely intended.

I took a deep breath, smoothed my hair, set my shoulders, and stepped into the kitchen, praying silently that I could keep myself from bopping Michael over the head with one of Grandma Jo's cast-iron pans.

Michael had removed his coat, gloves, and scarf, and he was placing the flowers, now in a crystal vase, on the top shelf of the corner hutch.

Grandma Jo stood by, smiling up at him. "Thank you, Michael. It's so hard for me to reach the top shelf."

"No problem," Michael replied. "Thank you for letting me into your kitchen to bake."

I cleared my throat. "I hate to interrupt the mutual admiration society, but we should probably get this show on the road." I gestured to the oven.

"I agree," Michael said, picking up his tote from the kitchen table and setting it on the island. He began removing items from the bag and lining them up on the countertop.

I saw a bag of walnuts, all-purpose flour, sugar, eggs, a little brown bottle of fancy Neilsen-Massey vanilla extract, a golden brick of European butter, a silver brick of cream cheese, half a dozen eggs, and a bag of snowy powdered sugar.

Without looking up at me, Michael began barking orders. "Bring me dry and wet measuring cups, mixing bowls in small, medium and large, a spatula and a wooden mixing spoon, measuring spoons, and a clean dish towel. That should be enough to get started."

"Please and thank you," I sputtered, crossing my arms. I had no intention of jumping at his command. Michael looked up, surprised.

"I was just trying to be efficient, no offense meant."

"Try harder," I told him, glaring at him and fighting the childish urge to stick out my tongue. Grandma Jo clapped her hands and stepped between us.

"Now, now, children. Please play nicely or remove yourselves from my kitchen." She gestured to the top row of cabinets over the toaster oven. "All of my baking supplies are up there, Michael. Please have a look around and help yourself."

While I stood and watched, Michael strode over to the row of cabinets, opened them one by one, and began rummaging around. I watched him remove a large mixing bowl and then begin placing smaller items into the cavernous bowl. Efficient, indeed.

After a few trips back and forth between the cabinets and the island, Michael pressed his hands together and rocked back on his heels. "Okay, I think we're doing good so far. Mrs. Morton, do you have a stand mixer, by chance?"

Grandma Jo smiled at him and pointed to the far corner of the countertops and Michael smiled sheepishly. He turned his attention to me.

Here we go, bossypants is about to go off, I thought.

"Miss Branson, if you're ready and willing, we may begin." With a little bow, he added, "Please and thank you." He glanced up at me from under those thick dark blond lashes, his pale blue eyes sparkling. My traitorous heart did a little kick-flip in my chest. I ignored the sensation and rubbed my hands together briskly.

"Sure, let's get to it." I rubbed my hands together and clapped them. "Do you have a recipe that you work off of?" I asked.

Michael looked at me as if I had just asked him if he preferred to wear a coat or a swimsuit for sledding. "My mother taught me to make these cookies as soon as I was big enough to stand on a chair and help her in the kitchen. The recipe is in here," he said, tapping the side of his head. "And in here." He tapped his chest.

I opened my mouth to make a smart comment, but before I could do so, Grandma Jo started to speak.

"That's where the real kitchen magic lies, in our hearts and memories. That's what makes food special, when it's made with love and care." She patted Michael on the arm and I could have sworn that, just for a moment, he looked misty-eyed. It was a fleeting moment, though.

Michael blinked briskly and grinned at my grandma. "Yes, ma'am."

I sighed and picked up a package of walnuts. "Shall I chop some of these up?"

Before Michael could reply, we were interrupted by the cheerful tones of "All I Want for Christmas" chiming from the apparently endless medleys of the holiday doorbell.

"Now who on earth could that be?" Grandma Jo murmured, heading towards the front door.

I turned back to Michael. "So I know you're really set on the kolacky, but I was thinking that it wouldn't hurt to have a backup recipe, just in case. I went ahead and picked up the ingredients for my cardamom sugar cookies, and I thought that maybe—"

"There won't be any need for that," Michael interrupted me brusquely. "As I've previously explained, this kolacky recipe has already proven itself to be a winner. My mom won the 2013 Allen County Fair blue ribbon for best baked good with this recipe." He began lining up ingredients on the countertop with an air of authority.

"I think you're being way too cocky about this." I leaned against the counter and crossed my arms. "What if something happens? You can't just put all your eggs in the kolacky basket, there's too much at stake here. Some of us really need this money!"

"That's right, I forgot that I was a secret millionaire and just doing this for kicks," Michael sneered, his voice dripping with sarcasm.

I turned and opened one of the lower cabinets and began removing baking sheets. I knew I wasn't going to win this one. I resolved to practice my sugar cookie recipe later, on my own time. Right now I just needed to get through this baking session. Maybe I would be surprised and the kolacky cookies would be mind-blowing. I mentally squared my shoulders and vowed to keep an open mind.

"A blue ribbon, eh? I'm looking forward to trying the finished cookies," I said, forcing a smile.

Michael's lips tilted up at the corners and his eyes danced. "Yep, I still have the ribbon. I keep it in a box of my mom's stuff. I'm hoping someday to be able to set her up ..." he trailed off.

I was about to ask him to elaborate when Grandma Jo entered the kitchen with Sheriff Weaver following behind.

"Hello, folks!" he boomed in our direction.

"Hey, Sheriff," I replied with a little wave. "If you came by to try some fresh-baked cookies, you're a little early. We're just about to get started."

The sheriff grinned, his brush-cut silver hair catching the overhead lights. "I came by to return Joanna's cobbler dish, but since you young folks are commandeering the kitchen this evening, I'm hoping that I can talk her into joining me for supper at the El." He used the popular nickname for the local diner, the El Royale.

The El Royale Diner was a relic from the 1960s complete with aluminum and formica tables and vinyl upholstered booths with glitter and space age star and comet designs abounding. The place was clean and in good repair, though, and served diner classics like meatloaf platters and patty melts that were reliably delicious and well-priced. The jukebox hadn't been updated since the 80s and I loved going there to enjoy a turkey club and tomato soup and listen to hits from Van Halen and Duran Duran.

Grandma Jo's cheeks flushed and her hands fluttered to her chest. "Oh, well, I suppose I could be persuaded to have a BLT and some sweet potato fries," she said. "Mikki, we'll finish decorating the tree when I get back."

The sheriff beamed and held up his arm, elbow out. "Wonderful! Shall we, m'lady?"

Laughing, Grandma Jo waved him off, giving him a playful swat on the arm.

"Let me grab my coat, Bob, and we'll head out." She turned to Michael and me. "And I won't be gone long, so no monkey business, you two." Wagging a finger, she winked and left the room with the sheriff trailing behind her, his shoulders shaking with suppressed laughter.

I busied myself with pulling the baking supplies out of the large mixing bowl, afraid to look up at Michael. I heard the front door open and close as Grandma Jo and Sheriff Weaver left.

"So," I asked Michael, "how long have you been in town?"

"About a year," he replied. "Did you grow up here?"

"Kind of," I said. "I lived with my grandma during the school year and all through high school."

"Are your parents dead?" he asked. *Typical,* I thought, *no polite euphemisms with Michael Brandon.*

"No, they're just performers. Theater people. They travel around the country with their troupe, performing plays and live shows. I'm an only child, so it was better for me to be here and have some semblance of stability."

"That must have been tough, growing up without your parents," he said.

"No, not really. They called and wrote all the time and I always had them in my life. I like being independent. It made me grow up stronger," I insisted. I looked up at him finally. "How about you? Any siblings?"

"No, just me. My dad traveled a lot for his career, so I was really close with my mom growing up."

"Wow, so you're on your own supporting your mom now. That must be really tough."

He cleared his throat and said in a choked voice, "Could I get a glass of water?"

Grateful for something to focus on after my grandma's embarrassing implication and a conversation that had suddenly become too intimate, I turned to the cabinet next to the sink and reached in to grab a lovely, old pressed-glass tumbler.

"Ice?" I asked without turning around.

"No, straight from the tap is fine," he replied.

I filled the glass at the sink, took a deep breath, and turned around to hand it to Michael. As he took the glass, our fingertips brushed and I felt a shock that traveled all the way up my arm and into my chest, jolting my entire body with a rush of energy that felt like a million little sparks flowing through my bloodstream. I gasped, and Michael jumped as his hand jerked and he drew back suddenly. The glass slid from our grasp and crashed to the floor, exploding in a flash of glittering shards.

"Oh my gosh!" I cried, leaping back from the shower of glass and water.

"Stay back," Michael said unnecessarily, holding out his hands. "Where's your broom?"

"It's in the laundry room," I said, heading towards the room off the kitchen. I came back carrying the broom and dustpan in one hand, and Grandma Jo's cordless vacuum and some old towels in the other.

Michael was pushing everything into the center of the room with paper towels. I handed the broom to Michael, holding the end and leaving plenty of room for him to grab the handle without risking our hands touching again.

"Get up as much as you can with this, and I'll go behind you with the cordless vac," I told him.

We worked together to get the water mopped up and all the bits of glass from the floor, not talking or making eye contact. *What the heck was that?* I wondered. I had never felt that sort of reaction from touching another person before. It was kind of thrilling, but also kind of terrifying, to have that much energy zap me just from making fingertip contact. *Maybe it was just static electricity*, I told myself.

Once Michael had shone his phone's flashlight across the floor and was satisfied that all the glass shards had been cleaned up, I took the broom and cordless vacuum and put them back in the laundry room. Taking a deep breath, I steeled myself and returned to the kitchen.

I was amused to see that Michael had found the supply of red Solo plastic cups that my grandma kept on hand for parties and barbecues and was sipping from one. I laughed and said, "Well, that's a safer choice, anyway."

Michael looked thoughtful. "I'll need the walnuts ground up, preferably with a food processor if you have one." He gestured to a bowl of nuts on the counter. He must have measured them out while I was putting away the cleaning supplies.

Okay, we're back to business. Good. I thought. "Sure thing," I said, pulling out the big Cuisinart and setting it on the island. As I began pouring the walnuts into the bowl of the food processor, I noticed that Michael was scraping cream cheese from the silver wrapper into the stand mixer's bowl. He followed with a knob of unsalted butter, a pinch of Kosher salt, and a dash of vanilla extract. Fastening the paddle attachment to the machine, he lowered it into the mixture and turned it on. I started pulsing the food processor, watching the walnuts swirl as they were minced by the whirling blades.

We worked without speaking, mostly because the mixer and food processor were so loud. Michael opened the bag of flour.

"Do you have a food scale?" he raised his voice to be heard over the mixer.

"No, not here. I have one at my apartment, of course, but Grandma Jo believes in baking from the heart and she won't use one."

Michael started to roll his eyes, looked like he thought better of it, and shrugged. "No worries, I'll just use the old-fashioned, tried-and-true method." He picked up one of the dry measuring cups. He scooped the flour in with a spoon and then leveled it off with the straight edge of a butter knife. He added the flour to the mixer bowl gradually, so that it didn't fly all over the kitchen. Once the flour was all incorporated into the dough, he shut the mixer off.

"Here you go," I said, holding out the roll of plastic cling wrap. Michael looked at me as if I were a dog that just blurted out a Shakespearean sonnet.

"How did you know I needed this?" he asked me.

"Hello, culinary school graduate," I replied. "I've made this type of cookie before, many times. I know that the dough needs to be wrapped and refrigerated for at least an hour."

"Correct," he said, and took the plastic wrap, tearing off a good-sized piece that he plopped the dough out onto. Once it was wrapped, he put the disk in the fridge and turned to me. "That will need to sit for an hour," he said, repeating what I had just told him.

"We can finish the filling, I guess," I said, gesturing to the ground walnuts. Michael removed the paddle attachment from the stand mixer.

"I'll just wash this, and the bowl, and we can get the filling done. Would you grab three eggs and separate the whites while I do that?"

I headed for the fridge. Soon, we had a lovely walnut paste made and nearly half an hour left for the dough to finish chilling.

"Would you like some more water, or maybe a cup of tea?" I asked Michael, desperate for something to do with my hands. I was still feeling awkward after our electric encounter and my grandma's implications of "monkey business" between the two of us.

"I'll take a soda, if you have any," he said, leaning against the counter with his hands in his pockets. He tipped his head towards the oven. "And we'll need the oven preheated to 375 as well."

I took a deep breath, pausing for a moment to pray for patience. I seemed to be doing that a lot around this man. I held out my hand.

"Give me the plastic cup. I'll fill it up with ice and grab a Coke for you."

He shook his head. "The can is fine, as long as it's chilled," he said.

"Fine," I said, pulling a red and white can from the door of the fridge and setting it on the counter next to him. I wasn't about to hand him anything anytime soon. Michael picked up the can, popped the top, and drank deeply.

"So," he said, suppressing a burp, "How long ago did you graduate from culinary school?"

"About two years ago," I replied. "I work at the Madison House Resort."

Michael whistled. "Wow, doesn't that place have a couple of Michelin stars?"

I shrugged. "I guess so, but I'm not the executive chef or anything. I mostly bake rolls."

Michael drew his brows together, taking another sip of soda. "Makes sense. You're still fairly fresh out of school. Plenty of time to work your way up."

"I also have a small cookie catering business on the side. I market on Instagram. Morsels by Michaela," I told him.

He reached into the back pocket of his jeans and pulled out his phone.

"What are you doing?" I demanded, grabbing for his phone. He easily held it out of my reach and continued typing.

"Hmmm," he said, scrolling with his thumb as he studied the screen, "Not bad, not bad at all," he said. "It appears you may have some talent after all."

"Gee, thanks. I don't think I can handle such high praise. It might go straight to my head," I said. "What about you? Do you have any culinary training?"

"Not formally," he replied, shaking his head. "I worked at a few restaurants and coffeehouses during college and picked up a few tricks here and there, and my mom was always an avid home baker, so I learned a lot from her growing up."

"How is your mom?" I asked, finally looking up to meet his gaze.

"The same," he replied, shifting his gaze to the oven as it beeped to signal that it had reached 375 degrees. "Let's get this dough rolled out," he said, sounding relieved to change the subject.

Soon we had trays filled with squares of dough that had been folded and pinched diagonally around logs of walnut filling. I slid two of the trays into the oven and set the timer for ten minutes.

"Those need nine to eleven minutes," Michael said.

"I know, that's why I set the timer to ten minutes," I told him.

"I guess you would know your oven best," he said with a shrug. He picked up the soda can and sipped from it. His gaze was on me, a speculative look on his face. Uncomfortable under his gaze, I started wiping down the island, which was covered in the powdered sugar that had been sprinkled liberally as we rolled out the dough and cut it into squares.

"Here, let me." Michael made a grab for the sponge and our fingers touched. I tensed up as I felt another jolt, but this one was more gentle, like a pleasant buzzing rolling in waves through my chest.

Michael left his hand on top of mine, and I could feel his breath gently moving my hair as he stood directly behind me. I was acutely aware of the heat coming off his body, which was almost touching my back. He smelled of cedarwood and sage, leather and wool.

I slowly turned around to face him. He was standing close to me, only inches separating our bodies, his arms resting on the counter on either side of me.

My heart was pounding out of my chest, and it sounded deafeningly loud. I wondered vaguely if Michael could hear it, too. I looked into the crystal blue pools of his eyes and then everything else faded away, even the thundering beat of my heart.

Chapter 8

*B*LEEEEEEP!!! The shriek of the oven timer blared as we leapt apart.

"Oh, uh, sounds like the cookies are ready," I stammered, my face burning with embarrassment. I grabbed the oven mitts and got the trays out, setting them on trivets to cool a bit.

Michael slipped two more trays into the oven without looking at me. I figured that he was feeling as embarrassed as I was.

Wordlessly, I transferred the hot cookies onto the cooling racks. They were golden brown and looked absolutely delicious.

"Time for the powdered sugar," Michael said briskly, loading up the sieve with the white powder and tapping the side to shower the warm cookies with a fluffy coating of snowy sweetness. "You have to do this while they're warm because …" He looked over at me and stopped when he saw the look on my face.

I wasn't keen on him "teaching" me baking techniques that I knew by heart already. But I had to admit to myself that the finished cookies looked and smelled wonderful. Unable to resist any longer, I reached for a cookie and bit into it.

"Oh. My. Gosh," I said, rolling my eyes rapturously as the light crisp buttery cookie and the bittersweet richness of the walnut filling burst over my tastebuds. "Michael, these are amazing!"

"Glad you like them," he replied, ducking his head in either modesty or because he was still embarrassed by our earlier encounter. His lashes lowered like silken feathers resting on his sculpted face, making him look like a fallen angel carved by some Renaissance master.

I swallowed the lump that formed in my throat and coughed loudly. The cough turned into a choking fit, with tears streaming down my cheeks as I gasped for air amid the strangled coughs.

Michael turned to me, concern etched on his face. He reached out as if to pat my back but pulled back and avoided touching me. "Are you okay? Do you need some water?" He peered anxiously into my red and streaming face.

I managed to gasp out, "Water!"

He grabbed the plastic cup he had been drinking water from and held it to my lips. It was oddly intimate, having him hold the cup to my lips, the cup that had touched his lips earlier.

I drew in the water, and the cool, clear taste flowed over my tongue and down my throat, easing the urge to cough. I closed my lips and drew back as Michael lowered the cup.

"Thanks," I croaked, pounding on my chest with my fist.

"What happened?" Michael asked, setting the cup on the counter behind him. I wasn't going to admit that I'd had some uncomfortable thoughts after experiencing the strong chemistry between us.

"Uh, some walnuts got stuck in my throat." I blurted out the first thing that came to mind.

Michael looked concerned. "I hadn't thought about that. What if one of the judges is allergic to nuts?" He looked stricken, and I actually felt kind of bad for him.

"I'm sure that a baking judge wouldn't be allergic to nuts, and if any were, they just wouldn't weigh in on those baked goods. It will be okay," I tried to reassure him.

He narrowed his pale sapphire eyes and looked me up and down, his expression cooling. "Convenient of you to bring that up, I'll bet *your* cookies are nut-free."

I drew myself up to my full height of barely five feet, two inches, and mustered all the indignation I could gather. "Are you implying that I'm trying to engage in psychological sabotage with you just to get you to switch to my recipe?" I asked, my voice rising to an irate squeak.

"I don't know, maybe," Michael said. "You do keep bringing up your recipe."

I didn't like the suspicious tone in his voice. "Listen here, buster," I said, "if I wanted to use my recipe, I would not resort to immature manipulation and games! I keep bringing my recipe up because it's my grandma's recipe, and I grew up with it, and maybe it hasn't won a blue ribbon, but it's a darn good recipe that you don't even deserve to have in your arrogant mouth!"

Michael's brows went up at my outburst. "Listen, I think we're getting off track a bit here," he began. His phone trilled in his back pocket. He grabbed it and looked at the screen. Turning away and striding towards the living room, he tapped the screen and held the phone up to his ear as he barked out, "This is Michael."

From the other room, I heard him murmur things like, "Yes, I see," and "Are you sure?" Finally he ended the conversation with, "I can be there in fifteen minutes."

I heard him coming back into the kitchen and quickly turned and busied myself at the sink, turning on the hot water and jamming the plug into the drain. The bubbles mounded up as Michael stepped up to the other side of the island.

"I need to leave as soon as the next batch comes out of the oven," he said, right as the oven timer beeped. I turned off the water and grabbed the oven mitts.

"Sure, whatever," I replied, yanking the oven door open and grabbing one of the trays. "I'm sure you think I orchestrated a scheme to get you out of my house so that I can secretly practice my own recipe." I didn't want to be petulant, but somehow this man brought out the fight in me.

"It's not that," Michael said. "It's my mom. She's had a rather bad day today, and the hospital asked me to come by this evening."

I felt my face redden as the heat of shame flooded my cheeks. "I'm sorry to hear that your mom had a rough day." I couldn't imagine what that might mean for someone suffering from a chronic illness. I felt like a perfect fool for being so petty and argumentative with Michael.

Instead of answering, he started lifting the cookies off the trays and onto the cooling racks with a spatula. Once all the cookies had received their powdered sugar shower, Michael set the sifter down and went to grab his coat and scarf.

"I'm sorry about leaving you with all the cleaning up," he said, shrugging on his coat.

I waved him off. "No worries, go and see your mom."

He headed towards the front door. I let him go without walking him out and heard the door slam. A cup of tea sounded wonderful, and it would give me time to gather my thoughts and emotions.

As I dropped the bags of Moroccan Mint into the teapot, I scolded myself for letting Michael get under my skin. He was a means to an end, a forced teammate in this baking competition that would give me a real shot at achieving the career goals and dreams that I had been pursuing.

If I wanted to truly live my passion, I just had to step back emotionally and treat Michael like a stepping stone on my path, nothing more. I couldn't afford to open my heart. Romance was messy and time-consuming and it would only get in my way. I had gotten this far on my own, and I would only achieve success by keeping it that way.

I poured the hot water over the tea bags, the clean and refreshing scent of mint rising with the steam. I inhaled deeply before I put the lid on the teapot. I turned to the sink to wash the dishes, feeling reassured by my newfound resolve. Just then, my text alert went off.

Pausing, I glanced at my phone. The text was from an unfamiliar number. It said, *"Hey Mikki, it's Tom Willis. Hope you don't mind, I got your number from Lacey. Just checking to make sure we're still on for ice skating tomorrow. Can't wait!"* There was a smiley face emoji at the end of the message.

Oh boy, I had forgotten about my "date" with Deputy Willis. This was exactly the sort of thing I should be avoiding right now, but I couldn't let him down in good conscience. That didn't seem polite, so I sighed and typed back a brief message. *"Hey, Tom. Sure thing, I'll meet you at the ice rink at 3 tomorrow. I'm looking forward to it."*

I briefly considered adding an emoji, but decided against it. Too frivolous at this stage in our relationship. I didn't want to get too flirty. It would make it complicated to keep things in the friendly space with Tom.

Almost immediately, my text alert pinged. *"Great! See you then! I'm really glad I ran into you today, Mikki."* This was followed by a winking emoji. I sighed again and swiped the messaging app up, closing it without answering. My simple little life had suddenly become very tangled.

Chapter 9

"**W**ell, that about does it," Grandma Jo said with satisfaction as she climbed down off the stepladder. She had just placed the glittering silver crystal star on the top of the fully decorated tree as the credits rolled at the end of *It's a Wonderful Life.*

I was exhausted, but Grandma had returned from her dinner with the sheriff bright as a new penny and she didn't seem any worse for wear after spending hours decorating the tree. The process took longer than it should have because she kept stopping to admire the old ornaments, telling little stories of past Christmases and reveling in memories. I felt a mixture of nostalgia and discomfort in those stories because they were all tied up with my fears of a lonely and bleak future.

"Grandma, can we clean up the totes tomorrow?" I asked, stifling a huge yawn. She laughed as she folded the stepladder.

"Of course, my girl. You look like you're ready for your forty winks!" She chuckled and clicked off the TV.

"I don't know how you aren't tired, Grandma," I said, grabbing the plates and cups from the cocoa and cookies that she had insisted we needed for "decorating snacks."

To my irritation, she had praised Michael's kolacky to the skies. But I supposed that it was a good thing from the perspective of having a winning recipe for the contest.

"Honey, when do you have to go back to the tent to practice?" she asked me.

I shrugged. "I guess I'll go in tomorrow during the day. The officials said we could go in by then." I made a mental note to get in touch with Michael to see if he was available to meet me at the tent tomorrow.

"When are you going skating with Deputy Willis?" Grandma asked me, glancing at me over the mountain of totes.

I smacked my forehead. "Oh my goodness, I keep forgetting about him. I'm supposed to meet him at the rink at 3 tomorrow." I really didn't need that complication right now, but I didn't want to be rude to Tom, especially after he had texted me to confirm.

I would go and spend an hour or so at the rink and then get back to focusing on the contest. I should have time to hit the tent for a few hours before I was due at the rink. I pulled out my phone and added a calendar event with a reminder alert so that I wouldn't forget again. While I had my phone out, I thought that I'd better go ahead and text Michael and get it over with.

Hi, it's Mikki. I was hoping that you might be available to meet at the tent tomorrow morning to get our booth in order and practice some more. Tent opens at 8am.

After a moment's hesitation, I hit the "send" arrow. After a few seconds, I realized that I was holding the phone and my breath, waiting for a reply. I forced myself to put the phone in my pocket.

"I'm hitting the sack, Grandma. I have to be up bright and early tomorrow." I gave her a kiss on the cheek as I moved past her towards the hallway that led to my bedroom. "Night, love you," I said.

"Goodnight, Mikki girl, sweet dreams," she replied as I disappeared down the hall.

Mrrow! I opened my eyes to see a pair of topaz eyes staring into my face. I rolled over, the desire to stay in bed overtaking all other senses. *MrrOW!* Acorn was more emphatic this time, nudging me with his head. I responded by pulling the blankets over my own head and groaned into the pillow.

I reached out and fumbled blindly for my phone on the nightstand and squinted blearily at the screen—6:15 a.m. And a text from Michael in response to mine from last night. The text had come in at 4:57 a.m.

"Hello. I'm on shift at the Java Hut this morning 6am–2pm. I can't meet this morning, obviously, but will come down during lunch to check on your progress. I trust that you remember how to make the kolacky."

I read the message twice. "Jerk!" I hissed and tossed the phone back onto the nightstand. Acorn looked at me in the dim light coming in from the hall and tipped his tabby head.

"Who does he think he is?" I asked the cat. "He's so condescending, somebody needs to put him in his place!" Acorn's ears went back, and he jumped off the bed and ran out of the room with a swish of his striped tail.

"Men!" I huffed, sitting up and swinging my legs over the side of the bed. I shivered as my feet hit the cold floor and I fumbled around in the predawn darkness for my slippers. I found them under the edge of the bed and jammed my feet into them and headed out to the kitchen, praying silently that I would be able to figure out my grandma's fancy coffee machine. I was certainly *not* going to show up at the Java Hut for my morning caffeine fix. I liked my coffee with caramel and cream, not condescension and bossiness, thank you very much.

Stifling a yawn, I filled Acorn's bowl with kitty kibble while he wound around my ankles and purred enthusiastically. "Eat up, kiddo," I said, patting his head. A scrabble of claws on the tile announced the arrival of Napoleon. The little dog ran up to me, his backside wiggling as he snuffled around Acorn's dish. Acorn let out a hissing growl and Napoleon jumped back.

"Now, now, that's no way to behave." My grandma Jo strolled into the kitchen, already dressed for the day in a pair of neat black trousers and a bright red sweater with a fuzzy white Santa beard adorning the front. Little Santa hat earrings dangled from her ears.

"Perfect timing," I said. "I'll make you a deal. If you make the coffee, I'll scramble up some eggs."

"Oh, no need for that. I'm happy to make some coffee and breakfast while you get dressed. I know that you have to get down to the tent this morning." She busied herself with the coffee machine. "Is Michael meeting you down there?"

"No, he's on shift at the Java Hut. He said he would *check* on me at lunchtime." Missing my sarcasm entirely, Grandma Jo smiled.

"How thoughtful of him to give up his lunch hour to come and check in," she said. Turning away, I sighed loudly and went to shower and prepare for the day.

When I returned to the kitchen, freshly showered and wearing my fluffy robe, Grandma Jo had a plate of eggs and toast, as well as a steaming cup of freshly brewed coffee, waiting for me.

"Mmmm," I said, sniffing the air appreciatively. "That smells wonderful, Grandma." I sat down and dug in.

Grandma Jo settled at the table across from me with her own plate. She picked at her food and seemed preoccupied.

"Everything okay, Grandma?" I asked between bites. She bobbed her head and took a sip of her coffee and then deliberately set the mug on the table with a snap.

"Mikki," she said, "I know you're making the kolacky for the bake off, but I wanted to tell you something about the cardamom cookie recipe."

I paused with my fork halfway to my mouth. Thoughts of recipe piracy flooded my mind.

"What is it?" I asked, setting my fork down on the plate.

"The original recipe goes back to my mother's mother," she said. "I don't know for sure where she got it, but she was the first to make them in the family. She made a version where she started adding sour cream to the recipe. When she passed the recipe to my mother, she added almond flour and almond extract. When I was married, my mother gave me the recipe, and she told me to add something special of my own to it. I added the cardamom. She also told me that when it came time to pass the recipe down to the next generation, I should tell them to add something special of their own."

She reached out across the table and took my hand. "Then, of course, I tried to teach your mama to bake, but she's never had any knack for domestic activities. She's always been a free spirit and a natural performer, just like her father."

A faraway look in her eyes, Grandma Jo continued speaking. "Your grandaddy was quite the character. He ran away from home at the age of 15 to join the circus, you know."

I sat up straighter in my chair, my eyes wide. "Grandma, I had no idea that Grandpa was in the circus!" It boggled my mind to think of the jovial man who had loved wood-working and being outdoors as a circus performer. "What did he do in the circus?"

"At first, taking tickets at the door, ushering people to their seats, set up and clean up, feeding and cleaning up after the animals, that sort of thing. Eventually, he worked his way up to the Ringmaster. Then one day, the circus came to Pinewood Corners, we met, and he decided to hang up his top hat and settle down. We got married and had your mama. Just as well, I suppose. The circus is rather outdated these days."

"Whoa," I said, "Grandpa was in the circus. I can't believe it. But I guess it does explain why Mom has such wanderlust and is happiest when she's on a stage."

"Yes, your mother definitely takes after her daddy that way," Grandma Jo said, squeezing and releasing my hand. "Anyway, the point is, I want you to take the family recipe and make it your own. Add your special touch to it."

"I can't imagine what I would add. That recipe is perfect as it is."

Grandma Jo chuckled. "I think it could always use a little something," she said, tucking back into her breakfast. "You'll know what's right when the time comes."

*   *   *

A short time later, I was climbing into Grandma Jo's Jeep, dressed in black jeans and a lavender sweater and my trusty old coat, my belly full of coffee, eggs, and toast. I backed slowly down the driveway, the tires leaving twin trails in the light dusting of snow.

As I headed towards the tent, I patted the bag next to me on the seat. I remembered the officiant saying that basic ingredients would be provided in the tent, but that any ingredients specific to individual recipes would need to be provided by the bakers.

I still had the supplies for the cardamom sugar cookies that I had picked up at the Fresh Stop, and I was bringing them with me. *Why not?* I thought. And then, because Michael Brandon brought out the most immature part of me, I defiantly thought, *He's not the boss of me!*

At the stop sign, I caught sight of my face in the side mirror and saw that I had quite a pout going. Laughing at myself, I switched on the radio. *Of course!* Grandma Jo had the station set on the all-holiday-music-all-the-time station. With a shrug, I gave in and sang along with "Last Christmas" by Wham!, belting out the 80s tune with abandon as I drove towards the town square.

There were a number of cars in the lot as I pulled in, and the big tent's windows were golden rectangles lit from within. I parked and jumped out, slinging my purse and the canvas bag of supplies over my shoulder.

Still humming along with George Michael in my head, I headed for the entrance of the tent. I breezed past the man sitting on a stool just inside the doorway.

He jumped up, almost knocking over his stool. "Miss, excuse me, Miss!" he rushed towards me, his eyes wide with panic. "I need to see a badge. You can't be in here unless you're a contestant!"

I skidded to a halt, mentally smacking myself on the forehead. I had forgotten all about the badge they had given me. I set the canvas bag down between my feet and began rooting through my cavernous purse.

"I'm sorry," I said to the man, who was now standing between me and the rest of the tent. I noticed that his badge said "Security." I kept digging through the purse. "I swear," I said with a nervous laugh, "this purse eats things and sends them to another dimension."

The man just continued to watch me. He didn't look amused at my attempt at humor. I finally squatted down and dumped the purse onto the floor and began to paw through the piles of papers and cosmetics and snacks that spilled out.

Finally, I spotted a red strip of nylon fabric wrapped around the plastic handle of a hairbrush. "Aha!" I cried triumphantly as I grabbed the fabric and pulled, revealing the elusive badge. I dangled it in front of the security guard's face.

He studied the badge for a moment then consulted a tablet he was holding. "You'll need to put that badge on and wear it the entire time you're on these premises, Miss." With a little bow, he gestured me onward into the tent as he turned away to go back to his stool by the entrance.

I slipped the lanyard over my head, careful to avoid hitting the bun on top of my head that I had tamed my hair into this morning, scooped up the contents of my purse, and shoved everything back inside.

As I stood up and looked around, I was hit with the smells of butter and sugar and cinnamon and vanilla, molasses and ginger and citrus. I inhaled deeply and felt a surge of joy. As I made my way into the tent towards my booth, I felt confident in my element as a baker. I approached booth 447 and as I stepped around the side of the counter, a cheerful voice greeted me.

"Hi there! I'm Colleen, contestant number 446!"

I turned to notice a pale, blonde woman wearing a red sweatshirt and jeans with a tan apron over her outfit. I smiled and held up my badge. "Hi, I'm Mikki—uh, Michaela. Booth 447. Nice to meet you." I hoped she wasn't a talker. I didn't want to seem unfriendly, but I had a lot to do and didn't have time to stand around chatting with her. To my relief, she simply smiled and turned back to her own baking.

Upon inspection of the booth, I was pleased to discover that the mini fridge under the counter contained sticks of unsalted and salted butter, milk, and eggs. The shelves under the counter held canisters marked with printed labels identifying granulated and powdered sugar, brown sugar, and all-purpose flour. A scan of the shelves behind the booth revealed other supplies, including vanilla extract, salt, and baking soda and powder among them, along with various sprinkles, chips, and candy melts.

I pulled out the supplies I had brought from the canvas bag; sour cream, cardamom, almond flour, and almond extract. To my surprise, a couple of oranges rolled out, too. *How did those get in here?* I wondered. They must have been in there from our trip to the Fresh Stop. I shrugged it off and turned the oven to 350 degrees to preheat.

After removing several sticks of butter from the fridge and setting them on the counter to soften, I started measuring out the all-purpose and almond flours and the sugars while I waited for the oven to finish heating. I was gathering up the oranges to put them back into the bag when an idea struck. The sharp citrus tang of orange zest would play well with the depth of spice in the cardamom.

Inspired, I started digging around in the supplies to find a zester. I finally spotted a long, thin Microplane grater. I used the tool to gently scrape off the shiny outer layer of one of the oranges, the bright and crisp citrus oils wafting up and awakening my senses.

After contemplating the second orange, I decided that the cookies would look more sophisticated with a swirl of candied orange peel on top. Peeling off strips of the outer zest, I trimmed them to quarter inch ribbons and set a cup of water and a cup of sugar to boil.

Before long, I had a batch of cooled cookies ready to be decorated. Humming as I worked, I concentrated on carefully placing a spiral of candied orange peel over the top of each freshly baked cookie, securing the peels with a drop of thickened simple syrup. I was just placing the last orange peel when a voice startled me.

"Wow, I didn't take you for a Wham! fan," Michael said from just outside the booth. I jumped, dropping the piece of candied orange peel onto the countertop.

"Sheesh, you scared me," I said. "I just have that song stuck in my head since I heard it this morning. I can't seem to stop singing and humming it."

"What are you doing?" He gestured to the cookies laid across the counter. "Where is the kolacky?" He pulled the blue beanie off his head and ran his hand through his blond hair.

"Um, I decided to give these a quick practice run," I told him. He didn't look happy. I continued in a rush, "See, this morning my grandma told me about how each generation of our family adds something to this recipe, and I was inspired to try adding some orange zest to the batter and some candied orange peel to the top of the cookies."

Michael studied my face. Without a word, he reached out and picked up one of the orange and cardamom cookies and bit into it. As he chewed thoughtfully, he examined the cookie in his hand. I waited, breathless, as he sampled another bite.

"Well?" I asked him, almost bursting with curiosity to know what he thought. He put the remainder of the cookie down, his pale blue eyes meeting my own hazel eyes.

"Miss Branson, my sincere apologies to you. These cookies are some of the best I've ever tasted."

I felt a warm glow spread from my heart all the way to my toes. I was absurdly pleased at how well-received my recipe was.

"But," he continued, "I still want to go with the kolacky, because it is a proven winner." I felt myself come crashing down to earth, my bubble effectively burst by his comment.

"You just said that these are some of the best cookies you've ever tasted," I said.

"Yes, *some of the best*, not *the* best," he clarified with a shrug. "Anyway, it's probably better if I'm here to practice the kolacky with you, so it's fine if you want to get a feel for the booth with a recipe you're more familiar with."

"Gee, thanks for your permission," I said through my teeth. "Did you want to practice later this afternoon?"

"Well, that's partly what I came to talk to you about," Michael replied. "The ice skating rink opens this afternoon, and—"

"Oh, thanks, I'm flattered at the invitation, but I'm meeting someone there already," I cut him off. Michael slowly turned an alarmingly bright shade of red. I could feel the awkward energy drift over us like a net.

Michael cleared his throat noisily and swallowed. "How nice for you. I was going to let you know that I'm not off at 2 today, as planned. I'm working a double because I have to run the coffee and cocoa booth for the Java Hut at the rink this afternoon."

"Oh, sure, of course," I stammered, grabbing a cloth and wiping the counter down. Embarrassed, I couldn't bring myself to look up at Michael.

"You know," he said, "I stood here and watched you baking for a while. You're very driven and focused. I like that."

"Mmm hmm," I said, still not looking up.

After what felt like a long interlude, Michael finally said, "Thanks for the cookie, see you later. We should meet here tomorrow morning to do a complete run through with the kolacky together."

"Sure," I said, trying not to sound as relieved as I felt that he was leaving. "See you here tomorrow at 8 sharp." I finally managed to look up at him.

He grabbed the remains of the cookie he had placed on the counter and held it up in a salute as he strolled out of the tent.

Chapter 10

$\int$ drove down Main Street, noticing that most of the merchants had fully decorated and lit trees in their windows, and some had cute themed scenes in the storefronts. Crawford's Hardware featured a scene of Santa's workshop, complete with elf statues wielding various tools and implements among a selection of antique toys. It was festive and clever.

I parked the Jeep and climbed out into the bracing air of the afternoon. It was clear and cold, and I could see the clouds of my breath in the air. I pulled my gloves on and tightened my scarf as I moved towards the entrance of the rink.

I sidled up to the back of the line of people waiting to get in, looking around for Tom. I spotted him further up in the line, talking with a gorgeous woman in a royal blue coat. I realized with a start that it was Rayna Reese he was talking with.

She threw back her head, her glossy black hair flowing down over her shoulders from under her fur-trimmed hat, and let out a throaty laugh. Her hand was resting on Tom's shoulder and he was grinning at her.

Tom turned his head and noticed me at the back of the line. He leaned forward and said something to Rayna, who furrowed her brows and looked back at me. With a smile and a pat of her hand, Tom stepped away to join me at the back of the line, leaving Rayna standing with scowl.

"Hi, Mikki," he said, giving me a quick hug. "I'm so glad you made it."

I hugged him back and smiled. "Good crowd," I remarked, gesturing at the people in line.

"Opening day is always crowded," he replied.

The sudden squeal of microphone feedback made us both jump and grimace.

"Hello! Is this on?" Mayor Reese's voice boomed out over the loudspeakers. His voice was met with applause and cheers from the crowd.

"Welcome, citizens and honored guests, to the grand opening of the Pinewood Corners Lights by the Lake annual holiday festival family ice skating rink! This year is shaping up to be the best ever for the festival. Come on in, enjoy some holiday fun on the ice, and don't forget to stop by the Java Hut booth for some refreshments!"

The gates swung open as the crowd cheered again and began to surge forward. Tom casually grabbed my hand as we flowed with the crowd towards the entrance. I stiffened for a moment, but relaxed when Tom gave me a curious look. I smiled at him, hoping that I was projecting a fun attitude. I really wanted to have a good time and forget about bake offs, mean girls, and handsome but arrogant guys.

Tom insisted on paying the entry fee for both of us, and we checked out skates from the attendant. As I laced up the ice skates, Tom grabbed our boots and put them in a cubby.

"Ready?" he asked, holding out a hand.

I took his hand and let him pull me up off the bench. We stumped over to the entrance to the rink and Tom stepped onto the ice, never letting go of my hand. I gingerly placed one skate onto the ice, then the other. I immediately began wobbling, and the more effort I made to stand still, the more out of control my feet felt.

"Steady now," he said, gripping my forearm and hand with his hands. "Grab onto the wall with your other hand, and lean on me with this hand." He gripped my arm tighter.

"I feel like Bambi," I said with a shaky laugh. We started to make our way slowly around the rink. I noticed a number of fellow skaters gripping the wall like I was.

The white lights strung over the rink twinkled in the late afternoon sun as we made our way around the rink several times, and I knew they would look beautiful at night, like winter fireflies glimmering over the ice. The crisp air was exhilarating, and I inhaled deeply. Holiday music floated from the speakers, and when "Last Christmas" started playing, I laughed.

"I don't know what's so funny, Mikki, but it sure is great to see you laugh like that," Tom said.

"Long story," I said. I realized that I was actually having fun, and I felt the tension drain from my neck and shoulders. "Thanks for inviting me, Tom."

"Of course," he replied, grinning. "How about we take a break and grab some hot chocolate?"

Tom carefully led me to the nearest break in the wall, and we exited the ice. We clumped along on our skates over the rubber matting that lined the outside area of the rink and joined the line at the Java Hut booth. The line moved quickly as we approached the counter to place our order.

Without warning, I found myself face-to-face with Michael. Somehow, I had completely forgotten that he had said he would be here today. And I suddenly became very aware of Tom's arm resting casually on my shoulders.

Michael glanced up and his gaze rested briefly on Tom's arm. Michael was wearing his blue hat and scarf and his leather bomber jacket, with a green Java Hut apron slung over the jacket. His nose was reddened with the cold. "What'll it be, folks?" he asked without missing a beat.

"Two large hot chocolates," Tom replied.

"Whipped cream and chocolate shavings?" Michael asked as he grabbed two paper cups and slipped them into insulated sleeves.

Tom looked down at me, raising his eyebrows. "What do you think, Mikki?" he asked.

"Yes," Michael replied, his ice-blue eyes boring into me. "What do you think, Mikki?"

"I think that sounds lovely," I replied, not breaking eye contact with Michael.

Michael served up our drinks with a flourish and Tom swiped his card to pay and left a generous cash tip in the jar on the counter before grabbing his cup and turning away to escort me to a nearby table.

We settled in, and I tucked my skate-clad feet under my chair. I swiped my tongue across the fluffy whipped cream crowning my cup of hot chocolate. I hummed happily at the sweet and creamy treat. The steaming hot cup felt good in my gloved hands.

"So," Tom said, "have you been enjoying your time in Pinewood Corners so far?" He sipped his hot chocolate.

I took my time answering, sampling my own hot chocolate. *Mmmm … rich, deep, and smooth … and not too sweet.* I wondered if Michael had made it before it was placed in the Thermos, then chastised myself for letting him occupy my thoughts while I was sitting here with Tom.

"It's always great to see my grandma, of course. And great to reconnect with old friends." I looked up at Tom, connecting with his warm and curious gaze. He grinned broadly and his eyes crinkled at the corners.

"How do you like your work as a deputy?" I asked him.

"It's been wonderful," he replied. His whole demeanor changed and he seemed to light up from within. "After I got my degree in criminal justice, I knew I wanted to work in a smaller town, and make a real difference in the community. When I found out that Sheriff Weaver was hiring, I was thrilled at the opportunity to come home and serve the community that I loved best. I couldn't ask for a better career."

"Wow," I said. "And all I do is bake." I tried for a light and self-deprecating laugh, and Tom gave me a reassuring smile.

"Mikki, your baking has a positive impact on your community, too. Baked goods make people happy, and they help people celebrate, and cheer folks up when they're down. You never know when a cupcake will absolutely make someone's day."

I blushed. "I never thought about it like that," I said.

"You're pretty when you blush," Tom said, studying my face intently.

I felt my face grow hotter with embarrassment. I glanced up and saw that Tom had set his cup on the table. He was beginning to lean forward. His hand reached up and brushed back a lock of hair that had escaped my wool beanie. He reached out and gently took the cup out of my hand and set it on the table.

As Tom's face began inching towards mine, I felt panic rising up in my chest. *Was he going to kiss me?* I jumped up, almost knocking my chair over as I nearly overbalanced on my skates. I clutched the sides of the table to steady myself. Taken aback at my sudden move, Tom jerked back in his seat.

"Oh my gosh, I *love* this song!" I cried. "Skate with me?"

Now Tom's brows lowered in confusion. "The Riley Motors jingle?" he asked. Too late, I realized that the loudspeakers were playing a commercial from a local business that was one of the sponsors of the ice rink.

"Um, yeah, it's really catchy," I said desperately. Tom shrugged and stood up, taking my hand and leading me back onto the ice.

"Whatever the lady wants," he said as I stumbled and slid onto the rink. We began making our way around the rink again as the jingle ended and Michael Bublé's velvety voice began crooning "It's Beginning to Look a Lot Like Christmas."

"Sounds like your song is over," Tom said, the corners of his mouth twitching with suppressed laughter.

"Well it was fun while it lasted," I said, and I couldn't hold back my own laugh. Tom let himself go and soon we were both giggling uncontrollably.

"Oh, Mikki, that was great," Tom said, wiping his eyes. "I can't remember when I've laughed so hard."

"Me, neither," I said, smiling up at him. Tom opened his mouth to say something, when I felt my body collide with something solid and warm. The next thing I knew, I was on my back on the ice, and the back of my head bounced on the hard surface as the strings of lights swam overhead.

"Oh!" I cried out and rolled over onto my side in a fetal position. Tom knelt down, his face filled with concern.

"Mikki, are you all right?" he asked. I looked up and saw Tom crouching next to me.

Michael of all people was on the ground nearby, seated on the ice with his legs splayed out in a V.

"What happened?" I asked.

"You're a terrible skater and you knocked poor Michael down," a throaty, nasal voice replied.

I groaned inwardly. *Rayna.*

"Mikki, do you need me to radio for an ambulance?" Tom asked, still crouched protectively over me.

"No, no, I'm fine. Just help me get up and get off the ice."

"Yes, she's obviously fine, so please move her out of the way. She's obstructing the rink." Rayna glared at me and helped Michael up.

He stood and brushed at the seat of his pants. "You okay?" Michael glanced at me and then at Rayna.

"I told you, she's fine. Come on, your break is over soon," Rayna huffed, grabbing Michael's hand and skating off, hauling him with her. Of course, she was as fluid and graceful as a swan on the ice.

Feeling even more like a total klutz, I struggled to my feet with Tom's help. He surprised me by picking me up and carrying me off the ice in his arms. His chest was warm and broad and he carried me as if I weighed as much as a feather. He sat me carefully down on a bench and began unlacing my skates.

"What are you doing?" I asked as he yanked off one of my skates.

"I think maybe we should take this date elsewhere, for your own safety," Tom said, starting on the laces of my other skate. He had it off my foot in no time. Tom smiled and patted my knee. "I'll go grab our boots. You sit tight." He was back a few minutes later, boots in hand.

I bent to yank my boots on, and when I sat up, I was blinded by a bright light shining directly into my eyes. "Ack!" I cried, squinting. "What's going on?"

"Just checking your pupils to make sure you don't have a mild concussion. Are you sure you don't want to go to the hospital to get checked out?" Tom asked, lowering his flashlight.

"I'm sure. I didn't hit my head that hard, and my hat absorbed most of the impact," I assured him. "If I start to feel the slightest bit dizzy or nauseous or anything like that, I'll go get checked out right away."

"Okay, as long as it's a promise," Tom said. "I'm hungry. That hot chocolate sparked my appetite. How about an early dinner at the El?"

I had a quick internal debate, and finally said, "Sure, that sounds good."

Tom grinned broadly and held out his elbow. "I'll drive and then I can drop you off at your car later."

I stuck my gloved hand into the crook of his arm, and we headed for his county SUV. I looked back and saw that as dusk was settling in, the crowd at the rink was growing larger.

As we headed to the diner, I sent a text to Grandma Jo to let her know that I wouldn't be home for dinner. She sent back a thumbs-up emoji as we pulled into the parking lot of the El Royale. There were plenty of cars, as the El was the best casual sit down place in Pinewood Corners to grab a bite to eat.

Tom came around the car to open my door and help me out of the passenger seat. "Don't want you slipping in the snow," he explained.

"Ha ha, very funny," I told him.

He held open the glass door of the restaurant and gestured me inside. The diner was warm and the air was deliciously scented with bacon and coffee. "Don't You Forget About Me" from the 80s classic movie *The Breakfast Club* was playing on the jukebox, and every table was full. The front corner of the diner was dominated by a ten-foot-tall, silver-flocked Christmas tree with pink and green ornaments and white twinkle lights.

"Hey, Deputy!" a cheerful voice called from the back of the large room. Tom looked over, waved, and placed his hand on the small of my back to guide me towards the voice. We ended up at the bar counter that ran along the front of the open kitchen. A smiling, plump, middle-aged woman in tight pink slacks and a vivid green sweater with platinum blonde hair done up in a tall twist greeted us.

"Hi, Darlene," Tom said. "Business looks brisk tonight."

The woman grinned, and bright pink plastic earrings in the shape of flamingos bobbed from her ears. "Sure is, and it's only going to get busier as the TV folks and fans come into town for the festival. Y'all going to sit at the counter?"

Tom indicated that we were, and she produced two menus and handed them to him. "Darlene, this is Mikki Branson. She's from Pinewood Corners, but moved away. She's visiting for the festival."

Darlene positively sparkled. "Pleased to meet you," she said as she winked one heavily made-up eye.

"Likewise," I replied as she moved away to help another customer that had approached the counter.

I turned to Tom. "I don't recall Darlene from my years living in Pinewood Corners."

"She moved here about three years back, and bought the diner from old man Crowder. She's a real force of nature, likes to joke about how she's worn out three husbands. I hear she's actively looking for husband number four." He smiled and handed me a menu.

I glanced at it briefly and saw that it hadn't changed much from my high school days.

Darlene came back with two glasses of water that she sat down in front of Tom and me.

"Decided on what you want yet?" she asked.

"I'll have the grilled three-cheese sandwich with tomatoes and bacon, and a cup of the creamy tomato soup," I told her.

She scribbled my order on an old-fashioned pad and turned to Tom. "And for you, hon?"

"The double cheeseburger deluxe and an order of fried pickles," Tom said.

Darlene dutifully recorded his order, ripped the page from the pad, and attached it to a carousel behind her for the kitchen to retrieve.

We settled in, sipping our waters and making small talk as we waited for our food to arrive. I was enjoying the casual atmosphere and the 80s music, and I had to admit to myself that I was also enjoying Tom's company. He was funny and kind and easy to talk to.

Before long, Darlene sat our food down on the counter in front of us. "Enjoy, kids," she said.

We dug in, and the hot melted cheese and toasty bread dipped in the steaming soup warmed me all the way through to my core.

"I forgot how fun this place is," I said as I stole a fried pickle from the basket in front of Tom's plate.

"The food is excellent, and Darlene runs a tight ship, so it's only gotten better since she took over," Tom said.

We were debating on whether to get hot fudge sundaes for dessert when I looked up and saw Michael approaching the counter.

"What are you doing here?" I demanded.

He looked over and took in Tom and I seated together. Without responding to me, Michael walked over to the cash register and gave his name to the waitress standing behind it.

Darlene came out of the kitchen with a large white paper bag. She grinned at Michael. "Well, if it isn't the prettiest man in Wingate County! I have your order right here. Two patty melts and one large order of fries. I hope you're sharing this with somebody special."

Michael smiled and his whole face was transformed from merely handsome to absolutely stunning. "You know you're my best girl," he joked, taking the bag from her.

"Thanks, sugar," Darlene said. "If only I were twenty years younger." She chuckled warmly and gave Michael a friendly peck on the cheek.

He turned to go and held up the bag, meeting my gaze directly. "I'm picking up dinner," he said, answering my earlier question.

I felt oddly upset that he had ordered two sandwiches and then I was annoyed at myself for feeling upset. I told myself that it was none of my business who he ate dinner with. I was on a date myself, for crying out loud. Somehow my mouth got away from my brain and my sarcasm let loose.

"Well, how nice of you," I said. "You might want to wipe that bright pink lipstick off your cheek before your date sees it."

Michael's eyes narrowed. He reached out and pulled some napkins from the holder on the counter and scrubbed the side of his face. "Thanks for the tip," he said, and he strode out, clutching the bag.

"He's got some nerve," I began spouting off to Tom.

"What do you mean? He just came in to pick up a food order," Tom said, looking puzzled. I swallowed hard and took a deep breath.

"I'm done, I don't really want dessert," I said, reaching for my coat.

Tom signaled for the check.

I was suddenly and unaccountably worked up and didn't know what to do. I fumbled in my purse, grabbed my wallet, and threw some bills on the counter. "That should take care of my meal and tip. I'll meet you outside," I said, and rushed out of the restaurant before Tom could protest.

*   *   *

I stood under the pine-wrapped light posts, leaning against Tom's SUV, taking in deep gulps of the icy air as I watched the exhaled clouds drift up towards the starlit sky. I saw Tom's tall silhouette approaching and tried to pull myself together.

"Hey, are you okay?" Tom asked as he hit the button on the remote for the locks and opened the passenger door for me. I climbed in and settled myself. I took my time pulling the seat belt across my body and latching it.

"I'm fine, I think maybe I just ate too much cheese," I said. "I don't feel so well all of a sudden."

Tom started the engine without another word and we pulled out onto Oak Boulevard and headed back towards the ice rink where I had left the Jeep. We traveled in silence and I was glad for once that the town was so small because it would be a quick trip to my vehicle. We were soon pulling into the lot by the ice rink, which was now completely full. Tom pulled the SUV behind the Jeep and switched gears to "park." He turned towards me.

"Mikki, I had a great night. Thanks for coming out with me. I don't know how long you're in town, but I'd love to see you again before you go." He began to lean over the center console, reaching for me.

"Do you think Michael was just really hungry, and that's why he ordered two sandwiches?" I asked, crossing my arms over my chest and staring out the windshield. Tom put one hand on my shoulder and caressed it.

"Mikki, did you have a nice time tonight?" His fingers toyed with a lock of my hair. I glanced over at him.

"If the second sandwich *was* for someone else, who do you think it was for?"

Tom leaned back into his own seat and placed his hands on the steering wheel with a sigh.

"Mikki, I really like you, but I think I'm not the man you want to be sitting in a parked car in the dark with," he said.

"What?" I said loudly. "No, it's not like that, I don't even like Michael Brandon. He's rude and arrogant and bossy and I'm only putting up with him for the bake off."

"Sure, Mikki," Tom said. I heard the click of the door locks being released. "Take care, I'll see you around." He gave me a sad smile as I opened the door and hopped out.

"Thanks." I waved and he waited until I was in the Jeep with the engine going before he pulled away.

I sat and watched until his tail lights faded from view around the end of the aisle. I pulled out my phone and texted Lacey. *What the heck is wrong with me? I always chase away the nice guys.*

Right away, I saw the pulsing dots of Lacey typing a reply. *I want details, let's have lunch tomorrow.*

I read the reply and texted back: *Sure, any place but the El.* I put my phone in my purse, backed out, and headed for home.

Chapter 11

I woke up the next day to a text from Michael. *I will be at the tent by 8:30am today.* Well that was a typical Michael Brandon text if I had ever seen one. No asking, no apologizing, no explaining, just a blunt statement. I checked the time and saw that it was almost seven. I jumped out of bed and rushed off to shower and dress.

When I entered the kitchen, it was empty. I saw that there was coffee in the pot, so I made a beeline for some much-needed caffeine. I decided on a to-go mug since I wanted to beat Michael to the tent this morning. On my way out the door, I poked my head into my grandma's quilting studio and saw that she was hard at work on the bride's quilt.

"Hi, Grandma. Bye, Grandma," I said.

She glanced up and looked at me over the top of her magnifying glasses. "How was your date?"

"It was fine," I replied.

She raised her brows but didn't push for more information. "I fed Acorn already this morning when I fed Napoleon. Where are you off to?"

"Thanks. I'm headed for the tent for more practice today. Michael is actually going to be there today, so we need to get some teamwork going."

"Have a good day, dear," she said as she went back to her quilting. "By the way," she called out as I headed down the hall, "I need the Jeep today, I'm meeting Sheriff Weaver at the Furniture Barn to help him pick out a new sofa."

I grinned and called out, "Okay!" as I grabbed the keys to my Chevy and stepped out the door.

*   *   *

The parking lot of the tent was packed, and I noticed that a large RV was parked along one side of the lot, along with several vans with the Culinary Channel logo on the sides. I felt a shiver of nervous excitement as I stepped through the front entrance.

"Miss! Wait!" The same security guard from yesterday stopped me.

"Don't you recognize me from yesterday?" I asked.

"Rules are rules, Miss," he replied. "No badge, no entry."

I went through the routine of dumping and digging with my purse. *I really need a smaller bag,* I thought as I finally extracted my badge and looped it over my head carefully, so as not to disturb the intricately curled and styled hair that had taken up most of my time this morning. It didn't occur to me to wonder why I had taken such care with my appearance this morning as I approached booth 447.

I was relieved that it was empty. I had managed to beat Michael here. I waved merrily to Colleen in the next booth as I stepped behind the counter and started checking on the supplies. I was pleased to see that everything I had used yesterday had been restocked. I was about to start getting things out for baking when I heard a commotion in the far corner of the tent.

"What's going on?" I asked Colleen.

She shrugged. "Must be the celebrity judges and the host arriving."

I was intrigued. "Who's on the panel? And who's hosting, do you know?"

Colleen leaned forward conspiratorially. "I heard that Ladd Bianchi is hosting! I just love his *Roadside Restaurants* show. The celebrity judges are probably other Culinary Channel stars. It's so exciting!" Her eyes shone.

I glanced over and saw that there was a crew setting up lighting and a woman wearing a headset and carrying a clipboard was heading my way. She stopped at my booth.

"Hi, I'm Carly, I'm a sound engineer with the Culinary Channel. I'm here to get you mic'd up for a sound test."

"Okay, sure," I said.

Carly showed me the little pack that would be attached to my waist and explained how it would be looped around and the tiny mic would be attached under my clothing. After wiring me and testing my voice levels, Carly removed her equipment and moved on to Colleen next door. She had asked that I have Michael find her for his sound test when he arrived.

All the contestants were showing up, it seemed. The booths around me began to fill up with people. At 8:30 a.m. on the dot, Michael strolled up to our booth.

"Good morning," he said. He was holding a paper tray with lidded cups in it.

"Hi, is that coffee?" I asked. Michael nodded and set the tray on the counter as he entered the booth.

"A caramel latte for you, and a flat white for Colleen here." He held a cup out to our neighbor, and she grabbed it like a lifeline.

"Oh thank you, Michael. You're so sweet, it's amazing how you remember all of your customers' favorite coffees."

"No problem," Michael replied, ducking his head. As he was removing his coat, a voice cut through the crowd.

"Michael! I need your help unloading some things!"

Michael's face went still, and he paused in removing his coat.

Rayna waltzed up as if she owned the place and repeated her request for help unloading.

"Rayna, aren't there any crew members that can help you?" Michael asked.

She narrowed her violet eyes. "I don't trust them. I have some delicate things that I want to use to decorate my booth."

"Sure, Rayna," Michael said, shrugging back into his coat. "Be right back," he said to me.

"Those two sure make a gorgeous couple," Colleen commented.

I glanced sharply at her. "What do you mean?" I asked.

"Just that they're both so good-looking, it's no surprise that they would find their way to one another. It just makes sense."

"So they *are* together?" I asked.

Colleen shrugged. "He was with her at the Pet Palace a couple of weeks ago. They picked out two goldfish together."

"Goldfish?" I asked her.

"Yes, I work at the Pet Palace, you know." I didn't know, but Colleen continued with her story.

"They chose the goldfish, and he told her she should name them Mary and Berry and she laughed. Isn't that cute? After Mary Berry from the Great British Bake Off? They also picked out a tank together."

"Oh," I said, because I didn't know how else to respond to this piece of news. "That's interesting."

Colleen shrugged and turned back to her baking. I decided to follow her example and began taking out ingredients and measuring them out in preparation for baking our kolacky.

Next thing I knew, there was a ruckus in the booth directly across from me. Michael was following behind Rayna, carrying several boxes while she barked out orders. I heard Michael say something about getting back to his own booth and Rayna shrilly informed him that she had to go interview Ladd Bianchi for the paper and she wanted Michael to begin putting up her decorations.

"It has to look like an old-fashioned Victorian kitchen," she insisted. I had no earthly idea why she thought that decorating her booth would make any difference to the outcome of the contest, but she seemed adamant.

"Look, I can unload your boxes and open them, but I have to get to work in my own booth," Michael repeated. He sounded as if his patience was beginning to wear thin.

I suppressed a smile as I sipped my latte and watched the show unfolding across from me.

"Oh, fine, I'll do it myself as soon as I'm done with my interview," Rayna huffed. She grabbed a recorder from her purse and slapped on her press credential badge alongside her bake off contestant badge and stalked off, presumably to do her interview.

As Michael approached our booth, I asked, "Everything all settled?"

He shrugged out of his coat and looked over the countertop. "Looks like you've got everything out already. Thanks."

"Sure," I said. "The oven is preheated, so we should get the dough put together and chilling as soon as we can."

Michael rubbed his hands together. "Let's do it!" he said.

We spent the next hour or so working through the recipe, hip to hip in the booth, sliding back and forth behind one another, falling into an easy rhythm. I couldn't help but notice how good Michael smelled, like light musk and cedar and sandalwood. His scent was masculine and clean. I was lost in thoughts of trying to guess what cologne he was wearing when I realized Michael was speaking to me.

"So I had to make sure that the hospital carries the Culinary Channel so my mom can see the contest live from her room," he said.

Thinking quickly on my feet, I replied, "Oh. That's nice." I could have kicked myself for sounding so inane. "I hope she's doing better," I added, trying to sound more supportive.

"She has good days and bad days," Michael said, as he covered the finished dough in plastic wrap. He popped the dough into the mini fridge and leaned against the counter with his arms crossed.

"How's Mrs. Morton coming along with her latest quilt?" Michael asked me.

"Fine, she was working on it this morning when I left," I told him. "I didn't realize that you knew about her quilting."

"Oh, sure, Mrs. Morton's quilts are famous around here. I'm a big fan of her work. I would love to buy one, if I could afford it. It would make my mom so happy to have a pretty quilt like that to brighten her room. Little things like that make a big difference when you're bed bound."

I smiled. "Maybe you can work out a trade. Coffee beans for a quilt."

"Yeah, free coffee beans every week for the rest of my life," Michael said with a rueful laugh. I gave him a friendly hip bump.

"Cheer up, I think my grandma would cut you a pretty good deal if you asked." I said.

He looked down at me and smiled.

My stomach clenched and my heart hitched in my chest. I mentally chastised myself for reacting so strongly. *It's just a smile, for goodness sakes!*

"Oh, I almost forgot, you need to find a woman named Carly to get a sound check done," I told Michael.

"Thanks," he said and then looked up at me, his blue eyes meeting my hazel ones. "So, did you have a nice time last night?" Michael asked. I was jolted by the sudden change of subject.

"Sure, skating at the rink is a festival tradition. Everyone around here does it." I turned away from Michael and started wiping out the sink. I was not going to discuss my love life, or lack thereof, with him. I decided to beat him at his own game. "Did you enjoy your patty melts?" I asked casually, as I squeezed out the sponge.

"Mmm-hmm," he answered.

Well darn, that doesn't tell me anything. I turned around to get the dish towel and saw that it wasn't where I had left it.

"Hey, where did the dish towel go?" I murmured out loud. Suddenly I felt a sharp pop on my hip. "Ouch! What the—" I looked up to see a grinning Michael holding the dish towel, his eyes dancing.

"Sorry, I couldn't resist," he said. I playfully swatted at his shoulder and laughed.

"You've got a pretty good aim with that thing, like *Lethal Weapon* but with towels," I joked.

Michael chuckled. "Yeah, too bad there aren't million-dollar contracts for the sport of towel-snapping."

"So are you saying you're the Michael Jordan of towel-snapping? The Tiger Woods, if you will?"

"Yep, best of the best," Michael said, making a show of polishing his fingernails across his chest.

"Sure, but do you have a blue ribbon?" I arched one of my eyebrows.

"Smart aleck," Michael replied, "Just for that—" His hand flicked out and I felt another sting on my hip.

"Ow! I guess I deserved that," I giggled and danced out of his reach.

I had just started cleaning up the supplies from making the dough when I noticed that Rayna was back, and she was dragging a tall stool around the front of her booth. I went back to cleaning up as Rayna started climbing up onto the stool with a large wreath in her hands.

Michael had begun pulling the food processor out when a piercing scream rang out in the tent. I jumped, dropping the canister of flour I was holding. The lid popped off and a cloud of white dust exploded. I started coughing and Michael ran out of the booth.

Through my watering eyes, I saw Rayna sprawled out on the floor of the aisle between the booths, her black locks streaming out around her. The stool she had been standing on was lying on its side nearby. Michael rushed to her side and knelt down.

"Somebody call 911!" he shouted.

"I'm on with the 911 operator right now," Colleen said.

Within moments, the area was crowded with contest officials and crew members and curious contestants. Everyone cleared the way as a team of EMTs rushed down the aisle with a stretcher. They knelt over Rayna's prone form and performed an examination. Rayna appeared to be unconscious as they strapped her to the stretcher and whisked her out.

Michael turned to me. "I should go with her, make sure she's okay. I need to call her father, too. I'll try to come back as soon as I can. The dough comes out of the fridge in 20 minutes."

"Of course," I said. "Text or call me with any updates."

He lifted his phone to affirm he had heard me, and disappeared after the EMTs.

I spent the rest of the morning dutifully finishing the batch of kolacky that turned out every bit as good as the ones that Michael had made. Pleased with myself, I checked my phone. Nothing from Michael, but there was a text from Lacey.

Hey future Culinary Channel star, how about Logan's for lunch? 11:30?

Logan's was the local sandwich shop, and I adored their Italian grinder. I glanced at the time and saw that it was after 11. I texted back that I would be at Logan's by 11:30 and began the process of shutting down and cleaning up.

"So I guess Michael isn't coming back today?" Colleen asked.

"Guess not," I replied.

"Any word on how Miz Reese is doing?" Colleen was lifting what appeared to be coconut cookies with bright red cherries dotting the middles from a baking sheet with a wide spatula.

"No, not yet. Hopefully we'll know more soon. I'll see you later," I replied as I gathered my purse and coat and readied myself to leave for lunch.

As I made my way down the aisle, I saw that all the other booths were full with bakers practicing their recipes. The rich smells of sugar and butter and chocolate and holiday spices like cinnamon and nutmeg perfuming the air were heady and delicious. I paused, inhaling deeply and closed my eyes for a brief moment. When I opened them, a man in a suit and tie stood directly in front of me. I recognized him from the day I had first come into the tent and he had told me that Michael and I had been double booked. Startled, I stepped back automatically.

"Pardon me," I said, and made to move past him.

"Miss Branson?" the man asked, looking at my badge to confirm.

"Yes, that's me," I said warily.

"We have been informed that Miss Reese has sustained a back injury and will not be able to continue in the competition."

"Oh, I'm sorry to hear that. I hope she'll be all right." I hesitated, wondering what this had to do with me.

"In light of the fact that there is now a booth available, we would like to offer you the chance to take that spot to compete independently, if you still wish to do so."

I was flabbergasted. Suddenly, I had the opportunity to compete for the full $50,000 grand prize. I felt some guilt that the chance had come about because someone else was hurt, but it wasn't as if I had pushed Rayna off the stool or anything.

I had a fleeting thought that I should maybe discuss my decision with Michael, but I rationalized that he wanted the full grand prize as much as I did. He would probably be more than happy to have me out of his way and out of his booth.

He probably wants to build a nest egg so he can court Rayna properly, I thought. *And goodness knows I could put the prize money to good use.*

"Thank you, I am sorry to hear about Miss Reese." I took a deep breath and plunged in. "I would love to take the available booth," I told the official.

He beamed at me. "Wonderful, that's great news! You will now be in booth 347," he said, turning his electronic tablet towards me. "If you'll just please sign here and here, and initial here."

He indicated with his finger, and I scrawled my name and initials with my fingertip as directed. The official thanked me and shook my hand vigorously before he strode away.

Stunned at the turn of events, I exited the tent and found my way to the parking lot. I had been too preoccupied to fasten my coat, and I shivered as fingers of cold wind crept up under the lapels. Low gray clouds had moved in and brooded over the parking lot.

I climbed into my Chevy and noticed that it was already 11:30. I shot a quick text off to Lacey right before I pulled out of the lot. *Running a few minutes late, but boy have I got some news for you.*

*   *   *

The lunch crowd was in full swing as I pushed through the front door of Logan's Sandwiches and Subs. The intoxicatingly comforting scent of baking bread filled the small cafe as I worked my way through the mass of sandwich fans packing the area in front of the counter.

I spotted Lacey sitting at a table towards the back. I was delighted to see that she had her daughter with her. As I approached the table, the little girl raised her green eyes to me and grinned from ear to ear. She jumped down, blonde curls bouncing as she ran to me and latched onto my legs.

"Aunt Mimi!" she cried. Mimi was Claire's nickname for me. She hadn't been able to pronounce "Mikki" when she was smaller, and it had come out as "Mimi," and the name had stuck. I ruffled her curls and scooped her up.

"Hi, Claire-bear," I said, giving her a squeeze and inhaling the fresh, sweet scent of her hair.

Lacey grinned at us. "I hope you don't mind. Jed's meeting me here to pick up Claire. He's taking her into Westlake to see *The Nutcracker* ballet tonight."

"Of course not, I love seeing Claire." I set the child on her feet and herded her towards the table, where we both sat. I noticed that there was an unopened sandwich on the table, along with a drink.

"I ordered an Italian grinder and a lemonade for you, I hope that's okay," Lacey said. Logan's made their own fresh-squeezed lemonade daily. Just thinking about it made my mouth pucker with anticipation.

"You," I said, pointing at Lacey, "are my new favorite person." I unwrapped the sandwich and took a huge bite, moaning in ecstasy.

"So what's this big news? And what in the world happened last night?" Lacey asked. "I've been dying over here."

Lacey waited impatiently while I chewed and swallowed, washing everything down with a swig of tangy lemonade. I glanced over at Claire, and the little girl appeared to be occupied with coloring the kid's menu in front of her.

"Well, you know how I was sharing the booth with Michael because we were double-booked?"

Lacey was breathless as she waved her hand impatiently in a *keep going* gesture.

"Today, Rayna showed up acting like the queen bee, barking orders at everyone, and she brought a bunch of stuff to decorate her booth. While she was hanging stuff up, she fell and the EMTs had to take her by ambulance to the hospital."

"What?" Lacey's eyes went wide. "Is she okay?"

"I haven't heard anything specific, but on my way out to come and meet you, an officiant stopped me and told me that Rayna has a back injury and won't be able to compete in the bake off. So … he offered to let me have her booth."

"And you said 'yes' right away, of course," Lacey said.

"And I said 'yes' right away, of course," I repeated.

Lacey squealed and threw her arms around me.

"Whoa, hang on a minute," I pushed Lacey's arms down. "I still feel kind of bad about it. I don't know if I should take the booth. I mean, Rayna got hurt, and I have no idea if she's going to be okay."

"Well," Lacey reasoned, "Why don't you stop by Wingate Regional after lunch and pop in to see how Rayna's doing? Maybe bring her some flowers."

"That's a really good idea," I said thickly through another bite of my sandwich.

Lacey clapped her hands in delight. "I just know you're going to win!" she cried.

Claire glanced up at her mother. "Why are you and Aunt Mimi so happy?" she asked.

"Because Aunt Mimi is going to win the bake off!" Lacey replied enthusiastically.

"Thanks for the support," I told Lacey, giving her hand a squeeze and sitting back. "Now, let me finish the rest of my sandwich, woman."

"Okay, okay," she replied, holding up both of her hands. "But you have to tell me what happened with Tom last night. Your text made it sound like it didn't go very well."

"Oh, it went very well-up until the moment when he leaned in for a good night kiss, and I couldn't stop talking about Michael Brandon."

"Uh-oh," Lacey said, leaning in for the good gossip, just like when we were dishing back in high school.

"Yeah, uh-oh is right. I mean, he's so nice, and he's cute, and we have some history and all that, but I just didn't feel that spark. You know what I mean?" I picked up my sandwich again and sank my teeth into the pillowy soft roll.

Lacey sighed. "Claire, honey, go and grab us some more napkins from the counter," she said.

The girl jumped up. "Okay, Mommy. I'll get you lots." She ran off towards the counter and Lacey leaned over.

"I know *exactly* what you mean. That's why Jed and I split up. We didn't have huge blow-out fights or anything like that. We just realized one day that we were living like very cordial roommates. The spark was gone. I suppose some women would be content to live with an amiable guy that's a good dad and a hard worker, but I just wanted more. I felt like I was too young to resign myself to a passionless marriage." She shrugged and poked her straw around in her cup.

"Well, it's not like I have anything going with Michael. He's obviously got a thing for Rayna," I said as Claire came running up to the table, her tiny fists clutching handfuls of paper napkins.

"See? I got you lots," she said proudly, dumping the crumpled piles of napkins onto the table.

"I see!" Lacey said, gathering up the napkins. "Thank you, you did a good job."

Claire beamed. "Can I color some more now?" she asked.

Lacey handed the girl her crayons and Claire climbed back into her seat and resumed her artwork.

"What makes you think that Michael has a thing for Rayna?" Lacey asked me.

I lifted one shoulder. "I mean, they're both super model gorgeous. Why would he look twice at a short, plain and broke girl like me when he could have rich and beautiful Rayna?

Besides," I held up my hand and continued before Lacey could interrupt me to protest, "I don't even like him, he's bossy and rude. Why would I want to pursue someone who isn't interested in me?"

"So what are you going to do?" Lacey asked.

"What I came here to do. I'm going to focus my energy on the bake off. I don't have time for romantic pursuits, anyway. If—when—I win that prize money, I'll be too busy getting my own bakery started to indulge in a love life, anyway."

"Sounds like a plan." Lacey held up her cup of lemonade. "Cheers to winning the bake off," she said.

I picked up my own cup and tapped it against hers. "And cheers to doing it on my own!"

Chapter 12

I exited the Fresh Stop with a cheerful bouquet of carnations and lilies in shades of pink and white. Fat snowflakes fell silently all around me, and I leaned forward to protect the petals from getting too wet. I climbed into my Chevy and switched on the wipers as I started the engine.

The snow was falling faster by the minute. I pulled away from the curb and headed for Wingate Regional Hospital. I glanced at the little bouquet on the seat beside me. I would have loved to get something from The Flower Barn, but the florist's offerings came with a price tag that was well beyond my meager budget.

My text alert went off. I pulled up to the stop sign at Oak and Main and picked my phone up off the seat. It was a text from Michael.

Rayna hurt her back. Doc says she will be fine if she stays off her feet for a while. Not able to make it back to the tent today. See you tomorrow morning. 8am.

A sharp honk from behind me spurred me into action. I tossed the phone back onto the seat and turned onto Main Street. The hospital was near the edge of town, where the interstate connected with the county highway. I drove carefully, my headlights on and wipers going a mile a minute to combat the relentless sheets of falling snow.

I was deep in thought. Michael obviously had no idea that I was offered the booth that Rayna would not be able to use. I wondered how he would react when he found out. I still thought that he would probably be relieved that he would no longer have to share the prize money.

The fluorescent lights were already flickering on in the hospital parking lot when I pulled in, despite it being barely three in the afternoon. The snowfall and low clouds made the afternoon prematurely dark. I grabbed my purse and the flowers and headed for the main entrance. A smiling woman with short, cropped gray hair greeted me at the reception counter. Her pastel green smock identified her as a volunteer.

"Can I help you?" she asked, looking up with a wide and welcoming smile. I pulled the hood of my coat down. I could feel the static electricity crackle around my head and I tried to smooth my hair.

"Yes, please. I'm here to visit Rayna Reese. Can you tell me which room she's in?"

"Certainly," the woman replied. She tapped on the keyboard in front of her and scanned the computer screen. "Room 218. Follow the blue stripe on the floor to the elevator bank, take the elevator up to the second floor, and turn right when you get off." She smiled broadly again.

I thanked her and headed down the hall, following the trail of blue as directed. I got off the elevator on the second floor and turned right, following the hallway and checking room numbers as I went. Just past the nurses' station on the right, I spotted room 218.

I approached the half-open door cautiously and quietly, in case Rayna was sleeping. I poked my head through the opening and saw Rayna lying in the bed, propped up on multiple pillows, her raven hair spread around her like sparkling black water, reflecting the light. Her lashes lay like dusky feathers on her cheeks and her full lips were slightly parted. Only Rayna could fall off a stool and be rushed away in the back of an ambulance and wind up looking like Snow White waiting for the kiss of life from her handsome prince.

I leaned on the door and the hinges creaked. Rayna's eyes fluttered open at the sound and she looked towards the doorway. "Well, hello Mikki. Come to gloat?" she asked when she spotted me. "I know that you took my booth, the contest officials already called me to notify me."

I edged into the room. The air smelled like antiseptic and laundry soap. "No, not at all," I said, "I mean, yes, I did end up with your booth, but I promise you, I never planned it this way. I'm so sorry that you got hurt. I never intended—"

"Oh, sit down. I know you had nothing to do with my accident. It's just a case of wrong time, wrong place," Rayna looked at me sideways. "Or the exact opposite, in your case."

I felt my face redden. "I brought you some flowers, to cheer you up." I held out the meager bouquet. Only then did I notice that the room was already packed with flowers, potted plants, balloons, and a veritable zoo of stuffed animals.

"How nice," Rayna drawled. "You can put them on the table over there, by the sink. I don't seem to have much room left."

I stepped over and placed the flowers next to the sink, almost knocking over a massive vase of pink roses. Attached to the side of the vase was a teddy bear clutching a heart. Above the vase and tied to the bear's arm was a heart-shaped mylar balloon that said *Get Well Soon*. I reached out and steadied the wobbling vase, and Rayna practically smirked.

"Be careful, I don't want anything broken."

"It's, uh, nice. Very cute bear," I replied, my stomach in knots as I wondered who had given her the arrangement.

Rayna sighed. "Could I trouble you to pour me a glass of water?" she asked. I rushed to the pitcher on the tray table. I poured water into one of the plastic cups and held it out to Rayna. Instead of reaching up to take the cup, she stuck her chin out slightly and parted her lips.

Did she expect me to pour the water into her mouth? Is she hurt so badly that she can't lift her arms? Oh my gosh, that's terrible!

I hesitantly held the cup to her lips and tipped it towards her. I tilted the cup too quickly and the water sloshed over the edge, spilling over Rayna's chin and down onto the chest of her hospital gown.

Rayna jerked back with a gasp and began coughing. She yanked her arms from beneath the blankets and shoved my arm away. "Oooh! What is wrong with you, you clumsy girl! Bring me a towel, now!"

Meekly, I ran into the little adjoining bathroom and grabbed the white towel that was hanging there. "Sorry, Rayna. I guess I'm not a very good nurse," I said as I handed her the towel. I was relieved that she seemed to have full use of her arms.

"Well that certainly didn't do my back any good," Rayna grumbled as she lay back and blotted at her chest with the towel.

"I'm sorry," I repeated. "I just wanted to stop by and see how you were doing, and tell you about the booth. And to see if you needed anything."

"The food here is horrific," she replied, "but Michael said he would bring me dinner later on, so I'm all set." Again with the smirk.

"Well, I won't tire you out then." I started edging towards the door. "Please let me know if there's anything else I can do for you."

"Some peace and quiet would be nice," Rayna muttered, settling back onto her pillow and closing her eyes.

I left the room, partially closing the door behind me. I felt I had done my duty, so why did I still feel awful? Michael had probably given Rayna a romantic bouquet, and he was bringing her dinner. The heavy feeling in my chest was confusing.

I had assumed that Michael was romantically interested in Rayna, so why was this confirmation so upsetting to me? Their love life was none of my business.

I took a deep breath, lifted my chin, threw my shoulders back, and strode confidently down the hall. I told myself that I didn't need the distraction of a romance, anyway. I could be dating Tom right now, if I had so desired. No more diversions, I vowed to myself. I would renew my focus on the bake off and throw my energy into building my future.

I was marching down the hall, head high, humming "Independent Women" by Destiny's Child, when I realized that I had turned right when I should have gone left as I exited Rayna's room, and I was now thoroughly lost.

I looked at the floor. Lines in blue, green, red, and yellow flowed over the floor in a crazy pattern, and I had no idea which one I was supposed to follow. I chose a blue line, since that was what I had followed to find the elevators the first time.

I was so intent on staring at the line on the floor that I didn't notice the two men standing in the hall until I was almost on top of them. I heard voices and pulled up short, just in time to duck back behind the corner before I ran into them. I was debating as to whether I should follow the blue line back the opposite way when I realized that one of the voices in the hall belonged to Michael.

"Isn't there another way? Some sort of assistance program that I could apply for?" he was asking.

"I'm sorry, but your mother's benefits are maxed out, and all of your avenues have been exhausted. There's nothing more we can do for her here other than make her comfortable. Your mother really needs to be moved to a long-term care facility where they're equipped to deal with 24/7 residential medical care. I recommend Briarwood. It's the best facility in the area for your mother's needs."

"I've looked into Briarwood. Without insurance, I would need over thirty thousand dollars just to get in the door." Michael sounded miserable.

I peeked around the corner. Michael was leaning against the wall, and his head was in his hands as he clutched handfuls of his hair. He looked utterly desperate, and my heart went out to him. The man standing with him had gray hair at the temples and he was wearing a medical white coat and had a stethoscope looped around his neck. He laid a compassionate hand on Michael's shoulder.

"I'm sorry. I wish there was more that we could do," he said.

Michael raised his head. "I don't want to have to put my mom in the state home." His voice was thick with emotion. To my utter shock, he started to cry. He bowed his head into his hands and soft sobs escaped as his shoulders hitched. The man I assumed to be a doctor patted his shoulder kindly.

Mortified at eavesdropping on such a private moment, I held my breath and silently tiptoed back down the hall, taking the first offshoot I came across. I couldn't even begin to imagine what Michael must be going through. Tears sprang to my own eyes at the thought of Grandma Jo being physically incapacitated and having to leave her at the mercy of the state-run home.

As soon as I was out of the main hall, I hustled until I came upon a nurses' station. I approached the young woman sitting at the computer. She looked up with an expectant smile on her face.

"Hi, can I help you?" Her hair was long and straight, caught back into a low ponytail.

"Yes, can you please tell me where the elevators to the main lobby are? I seem to have gotten myself lost," I said.

"Sure, follow the green line in the middle on the floor towards the vending machines at the end of the hall, and turn left. Continue down that hall, follow the yellow line, and you'll run into the elevator bank. Just hit the button marked 'L' and you'll end up in the lobby."

"Thanks." I gave a little wave as she went back to her work. In no time, I was stepping off the elevators into the bustling lobby.

As I stepped through the sliding doors to the portico over the main entrance of the hospital, I was dismayed to see that the snow was still falling swiftly and heavily from the darkening skies. I yanked my hood back over my head, cursing myself for vainly foregoing a hat today. My carefully styled hair would be ruined from yanking my hood off and on anyway.

I slogged through the parking lot to my car. Grandma Jo's voice played through my head, telling me how bald my poor tires were. Grandma was busy furniture shopping with the sheriff, Lacey was at the library until it closed at 6, and

I wasn't about to call Tom, considering how our date had ended. I decided that the only course of action would be to get into my Chevy, drive as carefully as I could, and hope for the best.

With a silent prayer, I turned the key and started the engine. I flipped on the heater and hit the defrost button. I sat for a bit, letting the car warm up and waiting for the defroster to clear the windshield. As I sat staring out the icy windshield, my thoughts kept wandering back to Michael, so heartbroken over his mother's situation. I knew only too well how it felt to be constrained by finances.

Finally, I latched my seatbelt with shaking hands and very carefully rolled out of the parking lot and onto the highway. The world was a wall of moving white. I clutched the steering wheel, leaning as far forward as I could, peering out the windshield.

Please please please, just let me get home.

I repeated this mantra frantically in my head as I crept along, the snow covering the windshield faster than the wipers could fling it away. I tried to turn the wipers to a higher speed, but they were already at the fastest setting. A pair of headlights drew closer behind me and the car began accelerating to pass me on the left.

In my panic, I hit the gas pedal harder and felt the car begin to slide out from under me. Not thinking, I stomped on the brake pedal rather than turning into the skid as I had been taught. The car slithered sideways and shuddered to a stop as it thumped into a bank of snow.

I sat in shock, listening to the wipers as they sliced back and forth. My headlights appeared to be pointing diagonally up into the sky somehow. I realized that I must have slid partway into a ditch at the side of the road. I applied pressure to the gas pedal. The back tires spun but didn't find traction. I tried again, to the same effect. I was stuck, and the snow was still coming down.

I was considering what to do next when I saw the glow of approaching headlights reflected on my hood. The vehicle stopped, and I heard a door slam. My heart pounded as I watched the figure approach in my side mirror, silhouetted against the headlights. Then Michael Brandon's face was peering in at me through the driver's side window.

"Mikki? What happened? Are you okay?" Michael cupped his gloved hands around the window as he looked in.

I rolled the window down and he stepped back. "Hi. I'm fine, just a little shaken up. I hit a patch of ice or something and skidded off the road." I felt some embarrassment at encountering him after witnessing his conversation with the doctor, but I reminded myself that he didn't know I had seen him break down.

"Why don't you shut the car off and climb out," he said. "I can call for a tow truck to pull you out."

Dreading the looming cost of a tow, I squinted in the lights at Michael. "Can you pull me out with your truck?"

"I don't think so, I don't have a tow rope." He started to turn away.

"Hang on," I muttered. I figured that having Michael help was better than a stranger that may or may not have good intentions. I shut off the engine, stowed the keys in my purse, and looped the straps over my arm. I climbed out and found Michael standing near the trunk of my car, his arms wrapped around his body. The snow continued to fall around us and the wind was biting cold.

"Come on, let's make that call from my truck," Michael gestured to me and I trotted gingerly behind him, trying not to slip and fall.

Michael's truck was black, and high off the ground on fat knobby tires. He approached the passenger side and pulled the door open. He made a come-ahead gesture to me, and when I reached him, he grabbed my waist and hoisted me into the cab of the truck. It was blessedly warm, and the truck smelled like Michael, woodsy and clean. I settled into the bench seat as Michael ran around the front and climbed into the driver's seat.

I glanced at him in the light of the dashboard. He was sitting there staring at me, with a look on his face that I couldn't interpret. Desperate to break the tension, I blurted out, "Don't you have to take Rayna some dinner?"

"How did you know?" he asked, tilting his head to the side.

"I stopped in to visit her, and she mentioned it."

"So that's why you're out on the highway headed towards town," he said. "I grabbed a sandwich from the place across from the hospital and dropped it off for her already. I was heading home when I saw your car off the road and stopped."

"Well, thanks," I said, finally looking up to meet his gaze. His expression was intense, his eyes an icy blue that seemed to glow preternaturally in the dim light of the cab.

"Of course. I wouldn't leave a damsel in distress."

"Hey, I'm not some helpless female that needs to be rescued, I'll have you know," I protested. I hesitated and then went on. "But I'm glad that you stopped. Thanks." I shivered involuntarily.

"Are you cold? Come here," Michael slid across the seat and put one arm around my shoulders and started rubbing my upper arm. "Let's get you warmed up."

"Thanks." I dropped my gaze and felt the slightest touch slide over my head.

"I like it when you wear your hair down, it smells nice." Michael's voice was husky.

"Thanks," I said again. My voice was a dry croak. *I was saying "thanks" way too much.* My heart pounded in my ears and I was suddenly way too warm in the close quarters of the truck's cab. My stomach fluttered and flipped and I wished that I hadn't eaten the entire Italian grinder earlier.

"I was thinking about the kolacky, and your sugar cookies," he said. "I think we should try making a test batch of your recipe together tomorrow, just to see how it turns out."

"About that," I said, intending to tell him about the booth I had been offered. I thought Rayna would surely have spilled the beans, but obviously Michael didn't know yet.

"Because I can't stop thinking about your … cookies," Michael continued, ignoring my words. He leaned in closer, brushing my hair over my shoulder. "I love how passionate you are about baking, Mikki," he said.

I felt the intense electricity crackling between us again. All the saliva promptly dried up in my mouth and I couldn't speak. My entire body ached with the force of the chemistry surging between our bodies. I looked up to meet Michael's gaze once more, and I found myself leaning into him, drawn helplessly like steel to a magnet.

His arm gently squeezed my shoulders as his mouth parted slightly. I could feel the tickle of his cinnamon-scented breath on my lips. My eyes closed as my own lips parted. Our mouths inched closer and closer together as my heart nearly exploded.

A deafening WHOOP WHOOP blared as the truck's cab was flooded with a blinding bright white light. I squinted, pulling away from Michael so quickly that I bumped the back of my head on the passenger window. In a flash, Michael was out of the truck and walking towards the Wingate County SUV that had pulled up behind us and was shining its floodlights into the cab.

I took a deep breath and tried to pull myself together. I could feel my face heating up with discomfort at how close we had come to kissing in the front of Michael's truck like a couple of teenagers. I felt sure that the occupant of the SUV had seen everything through the truck's rear window.

I smoothed my hair into place and was slicking lip balm on when Michael sauntered up to the truck accompanied by none other than Deputy Tom Willis.

"Well, well," Tom said, "look who we have here. I got a call from dispatch that a motorist reported witnessing a car sliding off the road and needing assistance, and it turns out to be you."

"Hi, Tom," I said meekly. *Could this situation get any more awkward?* I thought, wishing that I could climb into the nearest hole in the ground.

"Michael here told me how he drove past and saw you and stopped to help," Tom eyed Michael. "I guess he had to help you from the cab of his truck."

"Just getting out of the cold," Michael said, "I was going to call for a tow, but we haven't had a chance to do that yet." He opened the truck's door and gestured for me to exit. He stood back and allowed Tom to help me down from the cab.

"Well, there's no need to call for a tow truck now. I can push Mikki's car out with my SUV," Tom said. He stared at Michael for a few beats. Finally, Tom said, "You can move along now. I'll take care of her."

After a moment of hesitation, Michael shuffled back around his truck. With a wave, he got back into the driver's seat. He leaned out the window. "I had better get going. See you at the tent tomorrow morning, Mikki. Drive safe." Then he rolled the window up. With a roar of the engine, the truck pulled back onto the highway and rolled away.

I stood watching the taillights, wondering how all this had happened so fast. I felt as if I had lived through three days' worth of events in ten minutes. Michael was probably feeling ashamed that he had almost betrayed Rayna and wanted to remove himself from the situation as soon as possible. I was suddenly utterly exhausted.

"Well, let's get you out and on the way home," Tom was saying. "I'll follow your car back to town to make sure you get home okay. I'd advise you to get a good set of snow tires on this thing as quickly as you can."

In no time, my car was back on the road, and I was heading home with Tom's headlights shining behind me. The snow was lightening up now, and I made it to Grandma Jo's without further incident. As I pulled into the driveway, Tom beeped his horn and flashed his headlights as he continued past the house and down the road.

I let myself in, noticing that Grandma Jo's Jeep was not in the carport. I smiled to myself as I took my boots and coat off and patted a wagging Napoleon. *At least one of us is having a good time tonight,* I thought as I headed into the kitchen to heat up some leftovers for dinner.

Chapter 13

I strode into the tent the next morning confidently, waving my badge at the security guard near the entrance. He smiled and gave me a little mock salute in greeting. Proud that I had remembered to wear my badge today, I marched down the aisle towards my new booth. As I neared booth 347, I spotted Michael in booth 447, looking impatiently at his watch, and my good mood deflated. He looked up and saw me, and relief flooded his face.

"Hey, there you are! I was beginning to wonder if you were coming," he called out to me. "I've been here for fifteen minutes already." He stepped aside, expecting me to enter the booth with him. Instead, I approached the counter, staying in the aisle.

"Michael, I tried to tell you yesterday evening," I began. I swallowed hard and took a deep breath.

"Oh, here you go," Michael held out a paper cup. "Caramel latte, just the way you like it." He smiled broadly at me.

"Thanks, but I really need to tell you—"

"Here she is!" a voice boomed from behind us. "Ms. Branson, welcome." The officiant that had offered me the booth yesterday strolled up. "Have you had time to inspect your new booth yet? Do you require any further supplies?" The older man smiled kindly.

I glanced at Michael, who appeared confused, and rightfully so.

"I just arrived, but thank you. I'll take a quick inventory, and I'll be sure to let you know if I need anything."

The man looked satisfied, checked something off on his tablet, and hurried away. I could feel Michael's gaze drilling into me.

"What is he talking about? The bake off is tomorrow. You wouldn't defect the day before the contest—that would be insane." His eyes glittered as he narrowed them.

I planted my hands on my hips. "Insane? Why would you say that?"

"Well, obviously it would be a very silly move for you to try to go out on your own with such short notice. You wouldn't stand a chance." His voice was filled with scorn.

In an instant, my guilt turned into outrage. "Silly!? Excuse me, if I recall correctly, you were saying just last night that you thought we should try *my* recipe!"

At the mention of last night, a red flush crept up Michael's neck and over his face. "I can't believe this," he murmured. He turned away from me and dropped the caramel latte into the trash can. I stood there, stunned into silence at his behavior.

"Michael—" I began.

"It's fine, Mikki. I get it. You want to do it all on your own, you don't need anyone else. You've made that very clear. You got your wish." Without another word, he turned away and began pulling out ingredients and baking pans.

"Listen," I tried again.

"I just need some space right now, Michaela." Michael's head was bowed, and he didn't look up at me. He appeared to be taking deep breaths, and he was moving slowly and deliberately without looking at me.

Fine! I thought as I stalked over to my new booth, determined to move ahead. After a quick inventory, I got started on a batch of my cardamom sugar cookies, carefully adding my touch of orange zest. The process of baking did its magic, and I got lost in my enjoyment of the activity. My annoyance with Michael quickly faded. As I waited for the cookies to cool, I spied a canister of dark chocolate bars on the shelf at the back of the booth and felt inspired.

I broke the bars into a large glass bowl and melted them in the microwave on half power in thirty-second intervals until they were smooth and creamy and the digital probe thermometer I inserted read 115 degrees. I then added more chopped bar pieces, stirring them in, until the temperature came down to 84 degrees.

The sweet and comforting smell of the melted chocolate was like aromatherapy for me, and as I breathed in the delicious fragrance, I felt a deep peace and sense of confidence settle over me.

I reheated the mixture briefly until it came back up to 89 degrees. Satisfied that I had properly tempered the chocolate,

I carefully dipped each of the round sugar cookies into the bowl to coat exactly half of each of them in the bittersweet coating.

As I laid them onto the parchment-covered trays to set, I admired how lovely they looked. The cookies reminded me of the classic black and white cookies but with festive flecks of orange. The contrast from being half light and half dark made the final curl of orange zest on top stand out even more. My cookies looked absolutely beautiful, and I was pleased beyond words.

I turned my head as a group of people with cameras and lights and a boom mic approached in the aisle.

"Folks, we're coming to you live right here in beautiful Pinewood Corners at the annual Lights by the Lake holiday festival Christmas Cookie bake off. Today is the final day of rehearsal before the real deal hits tomorrow, and we're meeting some of the contestants."

A cameraman with a dolly trooped along filming as Ladd Bianchi spoke into a microphone. He was shorter in person than I would have thought, but his bright orange mohawk and oversized Hawaiian shirt were consistent with his signature look.

"The grand prize winner will receive a reward of FIFTY THOUSAND DOLLARS and a chance to film their recipe for a Culinary Channel special," Ladd continued speaking into the camera. He stopped directly in front of Michael's booth.

"Hey there, contestant 447, what's your name and your story?" Ladd thrust the microphone at Michael's face.

For a moment, Michael stiffened and froze like a deer in the headlights as he stared mutely into the camera lens. Finally, he said, "Hello. I'm Michael Brandon. I'm making classic kolacky." His voice sounded oddly mechanical.

"Fantastic, that sounds like an express trip to Delicious City! Is it your own recipe?"

"It's my mom's recipe," Michael replied in the same robotic voice.

"I'll bet mom's super proud," Ladd commented. "What's with the apron? MB Squared?"

Michael's face fell. His fingers brushed at the bib of the green apron with red embroidery. "Oh this? It's nothing," he said. He sounded self-conscious, but at least he finally sounded human. His eyes shifted briefly to the trash can and I spotted another green apron sticking out. I realized that he had had matching team aprons made for us and a wave of guilt washed over me once again.

"I look forward to trying them. Best of luck to you tomorrow, Michael Brandon," Ladd said before moving on with his entourage of crew members.

*   *   *

I was in the process of transferring my finished cookies from a red platter onto a white platter, trying to find a presentation that I was satisfied with, when the entourage crowded up to my booth. I looked up, and a woman with a headset and a clipboard pointed to her mouth and smiled, then pointed at me. I automatically pasted a wide smile onto my face as Ladd Bianchi stepped closer to my counter.

"Well, what have we got here? It looks like contestant number 347 has baked up something special. What do you call these?" He held out the microphone in his hand, and the boom mic hovered closer overhead.

The camera lens was a black and shiny all-seeing eye of Sauron, watching me and hypnotizing me. I stared into it blankly for a beat or two, and the clipboard lady made a rolling motion with her hand.

I snapped out of my daze and blurted out, "Cardamom orange chocolate dipped sour cream sugar cookies!"

Ladd did a mock jump back as if the name of the cookie had a physical impact. "Whoa, there! That's a mouthful. Mind if I have a mouthful of cookie?" He pointed to one of the cookies on the white platter.

"Please, help yourself," I gestured to the plate.

Ladd took one and he bit into it right in between the chocolate dipped half and the plain half so that he got a balanced bite. I watched anxiously as he chewed. He swallowed, put the rest of the cookie down on the counter and removed his wraparound mirrored sunglasses to look at me directly. He leaned forward, elbow on the counter, until his face was close to mine. His wide amber eyes stared into mine.

"Wow," he said. It was only one word, but Ladd said it with such emphatic reverence and seriousness that it was all that he needed to say. I blushed down to my toes.

"What's your name?" Ladd asked.

"Mikki—uh, that is, Michaela—Michaela Branson."

"Well, I don't think you'll need it, but good luck tomorrow, Michaela Brandon," he said with a wink as he began walking away to continue down the aisle.

"It's Branson, with an 's'," I said, but no one heard me.

Ladd was over the top in a lot of ways, but he was right. I should come up with a better name for my cookies. While cardamom orange chocolate dipped sour cream sugar cookies accurately described the cookies, it wasn't exactly the catchiest name on the planet.

Colleen, my former booth neighbor, strolled up. She was wearing a Santa hat and a green-and-white striped apron.

"Hi, how did you do with your first live on-air performance?" She chuckled and then continued without waiting for me to answer her question. "I babbled on and on like a fool and Ladd Bianchi had to say 'whoa, Nellie' to me to get me to stop talking, and it was SO funny!"

"I guess we're all a little nervous," I said. "Did you have any finished cookies for him to try?"

Colleen leaned in conspiratorially and whispered, "He said that my coconut cherry winks' texture was *on point!*" She looked pleased as punch, and I didn't have the heart to tell her that when Ladd Bianchi tasted something and then talked about the texture, that usually meant that he didn't particularly enjoy the flavor but wanted to say something positive.

"Wow, that's great," I enthused. Colleen beamed.

"Did you hear? They're announcing the winner live, here in the tent, on Christmas Day!"

"But the contest is tomorrow, on Christmas Eve. Why would they make us wait another day and come back here on Christmas?" I asked, confused.

"Ratings, I guess," Colleen said with a shrug. "I'm done for today, and we need to be out by three anyway so they can set up the spectator area for tomorrow. I'll see you then. Good luck!" Colleen bustled away as I waved. I quickly cleaned up my area and got ready to leave.

I glanced across the way and saw that Michael was still cleaning up in his booth. I took a deep breath and headed over.

"Need any help?" I asked. Michael looked up and narrowed his eyes.

"No thank you, I can take care of my own booth." He started to turn away, but then hesitated. He stared down at his hands and twisted the dish towel that he held. "Look, I'm sorry if I overreacted this morning. I just felt kind of blindsided."

"I know, and I apologize that you found out the way that you did. I kind of thought that you would have heard it from Rayna when you were with her yesterday. I tried to tell you last night, but—"

"Okay," Michael held up a hand to stop me. "We both did and said some regrettable things, I guess. Let's just move on."

We? I thought. *What did I do that was regrettable, other than not telling him sooner?* I felt that Michael's behavior had been more egregious, but I didn't want to point that out and damage the delicate bridge we were slowly building. Instead, I took a deep breath to steady myself.

"Well, I just wanted to say good luck to you. Now if you win, you won't have to split the grand prize money." I tried for what I hoped was an encouraging smile.

"I guess that's true. Thanks," Michael said. He finally looked up at me with his crystal blue eyes. "Good luck to you, Michaela." He winked at me and turned back to his cleanup.

Something about the way he said my full name, and the wink, made me feel a flush of heat course through my entire body. Fanning myself, I wandered out of the tent.

*   *   *

When I stepped through the door of my grandma's house, Napoleon greeted me as usual. I heard voices coming from the kitchen and headed that way. I found my Grandma Jo at the kitchen table with Sheriff Weaver.

"Here she is, the future bake off winner!" Grandma Jo jumped up from the table and threw her arms around me.

I hugged her back, breathing in her familiar lavender and vanilla scent. I felt comforted to the core in my grandma's arms. I reluctantly released her.

"Are you making meatloaf?" I asked, sniffing the air. My stomach growled loudly.

"Yes, I'm making turkey meatloaf with mashed potatoes and peas. It sounds like your stomach approves," she replied with a laugh.

"I think I forgot to have lunch," I said. "I've been baking in the tent since this morning."

Sheriff Weaver looked grim as he studied me. "You shouldn't skip meals, Mikki."

"I know, but I didn't want to break my stride," I said.

"Tomorrow is the big day," Grandma Jo said, grinning from ear to ear. "We are so proud of you, sweetheart. Bob and I will both be there in the stands, cheering you on." She waved her hand to indicate Sheriff Weaver. "And," she said, with a pause, "I just got off the phone with your parents. They're arriving tonight. They wanted to surprise you and come to the bake off to support you and spend Christmas with us."

I pulled out a chair and sat heavily. "Really? Oh my goodness, I haven't seen Mom and Dad since their theater troupe came through town with their production of *The Crucible*. I didn't think they would be able to get away this year."

Everything was suddenly blurry as tears wobbled in my eyes. I felt overwhelmed with everything that had happened in the past few days.

My grandma went to the stove. "This calls for a pot of tea," she said.

*   *   *

After a wonderful meal, Sheriff Weaver insisted on washing the dishes. I was drying them and Grandma Jo was relaxing with a cup of cranberry orange spice tea. The door chimed out "Santa Claus Is Coming to Town" and my grandma got up from the table.

"I'll get it," she said, hurrying towards the living room. When she came back, she was accompanied by my parents.

I threw the dish towel down and flung myself into their arms.

After much hugging and laughter and tears, we finally settled into the living room. Sheriff Weaver got a nice fire going in the fireplace and Grandma Jo plugged in the tree and popped the holiday classic *Elf* with Will Ferrell on the TV.

"Darling," my mother said, "we're so proud of you, we can't wait to be in the audience cheering you on tomorrow." She beamed at me and then turned to my father. "Randall, did you bring the gifts in from the car?"

My father jumped up. "Thanks for reminding me, Ellen. I'll grab them now!"

"Oh no, I don't have anything for you guys, I mailed them out a week ago to your PO box," I cried.

"No worries, darling, you just win that bake off tomorrow. That's enough of a present for me," my mother said.

My dad came back into the house accompanied by a stiff cold wind. "The temperature is sure dropping fast out there," he said, placing a gigantic shopping bag next to the tree. Several festive and colorful wrapped boxes peeked out of the top.

My mother asked what I was baking, and I explained that I was making my twist on the cardamom sugar cookies.

"Oh, I remember those cookies. Mother tried to teach me to bake them, but I burned every single batch," my mom said, laughing.

Grandma Jo grinned. "Your talents have always been on the stage, not in the kitchen, Ellen."

We spent a fabulous evening catching up until I glanced at the clock and realized that it was after midnight.

"Holy cats!" I cried. "I have to be up and out the door early tomorrow, I had better get to bed."

"Sleep tight, everyone. Tomorrow's a big day!" Grandma Jo said. She turned to Sheriff Weaver. "I'll walk you out, Bob."

We all went our separate ways, and I got ready for bed. I had expected to endure a nervous, sleepless night, but with the excitement and joy of seeing my parents, I felt a wonderful glow in my heart that eased my fears of the coming day. To my surprise, I was out like a light almost the moment my head hit the pillow.

Chapter 14

It was still dark when I was awakened the next morning by the sound of voices arguing in the hall near my bedroom door.

"She is NOT going to be seen in public in that—that *thing*, let alone on national television!" My mother's voice shattered the predawn silence.

"Whyever not, Ellen? There's nothing wrong with showing a little spirit, especially when it's a holiday-themed contest." My grandmother's voice was calm and full of reason.

"Why *not*?" My mother's voice rose with indignance. "Because I refuse to allow my beautiful daughter to wear a slouchy sweatshirt with tacky appliques plastered all over it, that's why."

"Ellen, you are being completely unreasonable. You're going to wake Mikki up!"

The voices faded as the duo wandered farther down the hall, arguing all the way. I sighed and rolled over. From down by my feet, Acorn gave an irritated *murp* as I bumped against him. He rearranged himself into a ball facing the opposite direction and I felt jealous that he had the option to go back to sleep. I knew that any further sleep would be impossible for me this morning.

Now that I was awake, my mind raced. The old expression "today is the first day of the rest of your life" kept playing through my head. The phrase held new meaning for me today. I pulled the covers up to my chin and squeezed my eyes shut.

I said a brief prayer that I would be able to bake to the best of my ability today, and that if it was my fate to win, that I would do so fairly and with grace. "Wish me luck, Acorn," I said as I rolled out of bed, squared my shoulders, and planted my feet on the floor.

*   *   *

I ambled into the kitchen a short time later, wearing jeans, my trusty boots, and a forest green sweatshirt. I had tamed my hair into a French braid that hung down my back. My mother took one look at me and smiled.

"Mikki, you look absolutely lovely. Holiday green without being tacky." She shot my grandmother a pointed look.

"What?" Grandma Jo asked innocently, her dangling holiday light bulb earrings flashing all the colors of the rainbow.

My mother rolled her eyes. "Mikki, I have something for you. An early Christmas present." She got up from the table and reached into her robe pocket to produce a small wrapped box. She pressed the box into my hands with an affectionate squeeze. "It's a good luck charm!" she said. "Open it!"

I tore off the paper to reveal a velvet box. I lifted the hinged lid to reveal a silver filigree snowflake charm on a delicate silver chain. "Mom, it's beautiful!" I cried. "Thank you!" I turned around and held up my braid so that she could fasten the necklace around my neck. It hung down over the front of the sweatshirt, standing out against the dark green fabric.

"I have something for you, too," Grandma Jo said, handing me a flat box wrapped in red and green striped paper.

"Thank you, Grandma," I said as I tore into the paper. The box contained a red apron with a green tie and neck strap and green pockets on the front. It would look amazing with my green sweatshirt and the snowflake necklace.

"Oh, Grandma, it's perfect," I said, giving her a hug. "I'm surprised you were able to refrain from getting something with glitter or lights," I couldn't resist adding.

Grandma Jo laughed. "You're so pretty, you'll stand out on your own. No need for all that bling for you," she said.

"Did you just use the word 'bling'?" I asked her, pulling back to look at her. She just laughed again, her eyes sparkling, and pulled me back in. My mom joined in on the hug.

"I think I'm too nervous to eat breakfast, but I could sure use some coffee," I said, pulling away.

"Oh, no worries, Michael stopped by and dropped off a Thermos of caramel lattes for you earlier this morning." Grandma Jo pointed to the kitchen island. "He also left this for you." She handed me the envelope that was sitting next to the large Thermos. I opened it with shaking hands.

Mikki, I wanted to apologize again for the way that I reacted yesterday to the news of you leaving our team. It's no excuse, but I had a bad day and I took it out on you. For that, I am deeply sorry. I suppose I felt threatened that the best baker in the competition was no longer on my team, but competing against me. No hard feelings. I hope that you forgive me. You're a beautiful, talented, and passionate baker, and you deserve every chance to win on your own terms. I wish you the best of luck today and in the future. Sincerely, Michael

I blinked hard several times and tried to compose myself as I folded the note up and stuffed it back into the envelope.

"What does it say, dear?" my mother asked, sipping her own coffee from a mug shaped like a Christmas tree.

"Nothing," I said, shoving the envelope in my back pocket. "Just wishing me good luck." I rubbed my hands together. "Now bring me some of that coffee!"

*   *   *

Between the two of them, my mom and grandma had managed to coax some toast and eggs into me. I fought back nervous nausea as I settled into the back seat of Grandma Jo's Jeep. She had insisted on driving us all to the tent. My dad reached across the back seat and patted my knee.

"Deep breaths, Mikki. Do you want me to take you through my warm-up before I go on stage? It's very effective for reducing nerves."

My mom turned around from the front passenger seat. "Oh, Randall, that's a great idea!"

"Thanks, Dad. Maybe later on." I gave him a sickly smile and closed my eyes. I drew in deep breaths and tried to calm down.

As we drove down Main Street, I saw that the street vendors had opened their festival booths along the sides of the road. The parking spaces along the sidewalks were closed to accommodate the booths that carried everything from hot cocoa and muffins to handmade gifts and ornaments.

The festival spirit was high, and the sidewalks were already crowded with enthusiastic shoppers. The weather was chilly but the skies were a vivid, crisp blue and the winter sun shone down on the festival-goers. The high school's show choir was setting up risers on the square for a concert performance of holiday songs later in the afternoon.

I had managed to find a semblance of calm as we pulled into the lot adjacent to the tent. We all exited the Jeep and my family wished me luck again as they went towards the spectator entrance.

I looped my badge over my head, grabbed my new apron, and headed to the contestant's entrance. The familiar security guard was seated inside the entrance, and his brief wave as I went past lent a sense of comfort that calmed me further. The tent was bustling with energy. People with headsets dashed around, and the booths were filling up with hopeful contestants.

*   *   *

As I turned down the aisle to head to my booth, I realized with a start that it wasn't the impending contest that I was most nervous about. I was nervous to see Michael. The realization had me blushing furiously with embarrassment as I approached my booth directly across from his.

He was there already, and his back was to me as he attended to something at the oven. He was wearing snug-fitting faded jeans and a green and red sweater with a snowflake pattern. He turned and saw me. I gulped and tried to smile. Lifting one hand in a wave, he trotted around the front of the booth and into the aisle to meet me.

"Hey," he said, "did you get the coffee?"

I smiled as he continued.

"And the note?" He raised his brows.

"I did, thank you. It was a thoughtful gesture. The coffee was just what I needed to get me going today." I tried for a friendly vibe.

"Glad to hear it," he said, smiling broadly. "So, no hard feelings?" He tilted his head to the side and raised one eyebrow.

"No, I understand that you've been under a lot of pressure lately," I said and left it at that.

"You have no idea," Michael replied, his blue eyes clouding over. He blinked and shook himself like a dog coming out of the water. "Anyway, I really meant it," he said, reaching out and giving my forearm a firm squeeze. "Good luck today, Michaela."

To my astonishment, he leaned over and brushed a kiss over my forehead. I was left stunned, standing in the aisle as he made his way back to his booth.

"Have you been fitted with your mic pack yet?" A woman's voice rang out from behind me, startling me out of my stupor. I turned and recognized Carly, the woman who had fitted me for a mic previously.

"No, I just got here," I replied as Carly hustled me into my booth and began clipping and hooking up wires to my body.

"Just do your thing and try to ignore all the cameras and the action going on, unless you're being addressed on camera directly," she advised. She finished her task with the speed of experience and moved on.

I began setting up to put my recipe together, lining up ingredients and measuring them out. As I was scooping flour into a bowl on a scale, a bright light washed over me and a boom mic appeared. Ladd Bianchi strolled up, wearing a Hawaiian shirt with a white background and palm trees with Christmas lights all over it.

"Hello there, Michaela," his voice boomed out. "How are things going so far today?"

"Oh they're going fine, thanks," I replied, my voice shaking slightly. I tried not to squint in the bright light.

"What's your plan of action?" he asked me.

"I'm going to bake the best batch of cookies I possibly can," I said. *Way to go, Mikki, what an original answer,* I thought as I mentally smacked myself on the forehead.

"Sounds like a plan," Ladd said and moved on. I wasn't surprised that he didn't want to stay for more witty conversation.

Now I was nervous all over again. I took a deep breath, concentrated on the feeling of the ground beneath my feet, and mentally pulled my shoulders down out of my ears.

Focus, Mikki. Just do the thing! I shut out all the commotion around me and allowed the act of baking to work its simple but powerful magic. As I measured and mixed, everything faded away and I felt safe and secure in my own little world.

A horn blared, startling me out of my baking zone. "Two hours left, bakers, two hours left until it's go time!" Ladd Bianchi's voice boomed out over the loudspeakers.

I assessed my progress. I had the cookies baked off, and they were cooling on racks. I had the candied orange peels ready for decorating the finished cookies. All I had to do was melt and temper the chocolate, dip the cookies, add the orange peel, and plate them for presentation. I felt confident that I was in a good spot to finish up well before the final buzzer.

I glanced over at Michael's booth. He was standing at the back, leaning against the counter and typing on his phone. His cookies were probably still in the oven because his dough required chilling.

I saw that Colleen was removing trays from her oven and setting them on the counter, so she appeared to be in a good spot as well. I smiled at her outfit, a Mrs. Claus costume complete with a wig and wire-framed glasses. *Well, she certainly looks like a cookie expert in that getup,* I thought.

I heard a male voice say, "I brought you a visitor!" and turned my head to see Mayor Reese pushing a wheelchair in front of him.

Rayna sat in the wheelchair, looking as regal as if it were a throne on wheels. She beamed at Michael. She was wearing a cream-colored sweater dress that looked like cashmere. Her hair was held up at the sides with glittering combs, her makeup was flawless, and for someone who just got out of the hospital, she looked amazing.

"Hi, honey," she wiggled her fingers at Michael.

He smiled warmly. "Hi, Mayor Reese. Rayna." He grinned at both of them. "How are you feeling?"

"Well, the doctors wanted me to stay in the hospital for a few more days, but I simply had to be here today to see you compete," she replied.

"I'm glad you could make it. Did they give you a front-row seat?" he asked.

"Of course," Rayna said, batting her long lashes at him. The oven timer beeped loudly behind Michael. He winked at Rayna and smiled again, his face lighting up.

"Thanks for coming by," he said. "Gotta get my cookies out!" He turned to remove his cookies from the oven.

"Good luck!" Rayna called out as her father wheeled her away down the aisle.

I felt sick inside. I had plenty of circumstantial evidence that Michael and Rayna were together, but seeing him smile at her like that was more direct, and the pain that I felt was sharp and surprising.

As Michael was setting his baking sheets on the counter, Ladd and the crew trooped up to his booth. "Hi there, how's everything in booth 447?" Ladd asked.

"Just taking my kolacky out of the oven," Michael said, his voice tinged with pride.

"Your mom's recipe, right?" Ladd inquired. "Is she here today?"

"She couldn't be here in person, but she's watching the live broadcast," Michael said. He turned directly to the camera and waved. "Hi, Mom! I love you!"

"Well, there you have it, Mom's recipe wins every time, right?" Ladd grinned.

"I hope so," Michael replied. Ladd moved on and Michael got out a sifter and the canister of powdered sugar.

I was about to start breaking up the bittersweet chocolate bars to start the tempering process when I heard a woman call out. I looked up and saw Lacey with Claire on her hip. I grinned at them. "Hi, guys! How did you get over here without a badge?"

"Oh, I have my ways," Lacey said with a wink. Lacey set Claire down and the little girl ran straight to me, throwing her little arms around my legs and squeezing.

"Aunt Mimi! I want a cookie!" she shouted.

"Honey, the cookies are for the judges," Lacey told her.

"What's a judge?" Claire asked as she looked up at me.

"A judge is a person who tastes all the cookies and decides which one is the best," I told her. She tipped her head to the side and contemplated what I had said.

"I wanna be a judge when I grow up, so I can eat lots of cookies too," she said. Lacey and I both laughed.

"Well, I guess we'd better start saving for law school," Lacey said with a grin. "How's it going with the baking?" she asked me.

"I'm in a pretty good spot, I just need to temper the chocolate and decorate the cookies."

"Chocolate?" Lacey asked. "I don't remember those cookies having any chocolate."

"I added it. Chocolate and orange zest," I told her. She rolled her eyes rapturously.

"Okay, I want to be a judge when I grow up, too."

I laughed at her silliness. "Thanks for coming by, I needed the distraction. I'm surprised my folks haven't tried to barrel into my booth yet."

"I saw your family over in the spectator's area. We chatted for a while. Your grandma has been keeping them corralled over there so as not to distract you," Lacey informed me.

"Well, thank goodness for small miracles," I said. "I love them, but my parents tend to steal the show wherever they go."

"That's the truth," Lacey agreed. "We'll let you get back to work. I just wanted to say hi and wish you luck." She grabbed Claire's hand, and they both waved as they strolled away.

I prepared my chocolate and got all the cookies dipped and decorated with a curl of candied orange peel. I had just finished plating the best-looking cookies onto a silver platter with a white paper doily when I heard the 30-minute warning announced.

A man with a headset and clipboard hurried up to me. "We need you to have your tray ready to carry over to the judges as soon as the buzzer goes off. We're sending you up for judging in alphabetical order by last name," he informed me. "The judging table is located at the north end of the tent. You'll need to set this placard up on the table in front of the platter you're presenting to the judges." He handed me a folded card with the number 347 printed on it in big, bold font. I took the card and he rushed away.

Alphabetical order by last name—that meant that I would be walking up right behind Michael. I shuddered and took a swig of water from the bottle at my elbow.

The final buzzer blasted out over the tent. Ladd Bianchi's voice flowed from the speakers. "Bakers, your time is up. Whisks and spatulas down, bakers, your time is up!"

The man with the clipboard returned and gestured to Michael. Then, as he entered the aisle carrying a tray, he gestured to me. I picked up my tray and followed after Michael. My mind raced with visions of me dropping the platter or tripping and falling down, taking Michael out with me. I shrugged off the negative thoughts and concentrated on putting one foot in front of the other and making my way to the judge's table.

Michael was just setting his platter of kolacky down on the judge's table as I walked up. I recognized all four of the judges from various Culinary Channel shows and contests. My hands trembled as I put my tray down and stood the card with my booth number in front of the tray and stepped back. My mouth felt like the Sahara Desert.

I clasped my hands behind my back to keep from nervously working them as I took my place in line facing the judges. Michael was to my left, and there were two women on his left. One of the women was Colleen, the other I didn't recognize. I was last in the line. The judges tasted the cookies in turn, scribbling notes on pads in front of them. Finally, they looked up and surveyed us.

"Wonderful costume! Cherry winks can be tough to pull off. What made you choose to bake them?" the male judge asked Colleen.

"Well I just love them, I always have. When I was a little girl, my dad would take me out on Saturdays and we'd always stop at this little bakery that was in Collinsville … or maybe it was in Rayton …" Colleen trailed off.

One of the female judges, a breathtakingly gorgeous woman with caramel-colored hair and big blue eyes who was famous for her Italian recipes, said, "Your cookies were a bit on the dense side, and you included a lot of extremely sweet elements. It was a lot for me."

"I agree," the second female judge, an older heavyset woman with a blunt bob, said. "The texture was off, I'm not getting any crunch from the cornflakes, and the single cherry on top isn't doing it for me."

"I liked them. The flavors are sweet, but they work together well," the final judge said. She was a lovely, middle-aged southern woman with a honeyed drawl.

"Thank you, contestant 446, AKA Mrs. Claus," the male judge said. "Moving on, the fruitcake cookies were about what you would expect from fruitcake cookies." The other judges agreed, and their comments didn't seem super positive. The contestant, a wispy blonde, looked crestfallen. The judges moved on to Michael's cookies.

"Now these," the male judge said, nibbling, "are a delicious example of a classic kolacky recipe."

"Thank you," Michael said modestly. "It's my mother's recipe. I'm here to make her proud."

"I'm sure that you have, because the textures and flavors in these cookies just sing," the older female judge said.

"Yes, the pastry is light and crisp, and the walnuts have just the right amount of sweetness," the southern judge concurred.

The third woman agreed. "Simply delicious," she said.

"Thank you, judges," Michael said.

The judges moved on to my entry. They nibbled and tasted and broke the cookies to test the tempering of the chocolate.

"Contestant 347, what do you call your cookies?" the male judge asked me. Caught off guard, I stood there mutely. Time seemed to stretch on forever as I frantically searched my brain for any words at all.

"Uh—chocolate orange cardamom delights," I finally said.

"Well, whatever you call them, they are melt-in-your-mouth delightful," the southern judge declared.

"The texture is perfect, and the flavors play well together," another judge said, adding, "The only criticism I have, if I'm forced to come up with one, is that the chocolate coating could be a touch thinner."

"Absolutely perfect, the touch of orange adds a bitter note that balances the spice from the cardamom. Well done," the male judge said.

"Thank you," I squeaked out.

Yet another man with a clipboard gestured from off camera for us to move along as the next group approached for judging. Another crew member pushed a cart up to the judging table and removed the trays to clear the way for the next batch.

As we filed away from the judge's table, Michael reached over and squeezed my shoulders. "Great job," he said.

I smiled at him. "Thanks. You too." It was a lame thing to say, but I was too overwhelmed to come up with anything more clever.

We waited in our booths for all the remaining contestants to run the tasting and judging gauntlet. Finally, Ladd Bianchi stepped in front of the cameras again.

"Folks, it's been an exciting day here in the tent at the Pinewood Corners annual holiday cookie bake off. Our judges have tasted all of the cookie creations and now they face the daunting task of tabulating all the scores and deciding which one of these bakers will be lucky enough—and talented enough—to win the grand prize of FIFTY THOUSAND DOLLARS and a chance to bake their cookies on a Culinary Channel holiday special. Be sure to tune in tomorrow as we announce the winner LIVE right here on the Culinary Channel!"

The lights cut off and Ladd handed his mic to an assistant as he was handed a bottle of water.

"That's a wrap!" somebody yelled and a bell clanged.

The contestants were told that the top five finalists would be notified that evening that they would need to return to the tent tomorrow for the announcement of the grand prize winner. If we didn't receive a call, we could assume that we were not finalists, but we were welcome to come to observe as audience members. With that, we were all dismissed.

I caught up with my family in the parking lot and I was swallowed up in a giant group hug.

"Oh darling, I'm so proud of you," my mother cried.

"Well done." My father patted me on the back.

"I knew you could do it!" Grandma Jo said.

"I haven't done anything yet," I said, and I explained to them that I would need to wait for a call from the production team to find out if I was a finalist. My family assured me that they had the utmost confidence in me, and we piled into the Jeep to head home and wait.

I got up and paced the floor for the hundredth time. At least, it felt like the hundredth time. "It's already six o'clock! They're not going to call. I didn't make it."

"Mikki, darling, calm down. It's barely been an hour. Give it more time," my mother said in a soothing tone from the couch. "Sit down and watch *Christmas Vacation* with me." She patted the cushion next to her.

"I can't sit, Mom, I'm too keyed up," I told her. "I'm going to go and see if Grandma Jo needs any help in the kitchen."

My grandmother looked up from the pot of sauce she was stirring on the stove. "Can't sit still, eh?" she asked.

"No," I replied, "I came in here to see if you needed any help. Mom's watching a movie and Dad is napping."

Grandma Jo took pity on me. "Why don't you make the garlic bread?" she offered, gesturing to the baguette on the island. Relieved to have something to occupy my hands and my brain, I grabbed the bread, took a large serrated knife, and sliced it in half long-ways.

I snagged some basil and oregano from the potted herbs in the windowsill and tore them up, then I roughly chopped lots of fresh garlic and put the herbs and garlic into the sturdy ceramic mortar along with a generous pinch of Kosher salt and ground everything together with the pestle. Then I melted a stick of butter over low heat in a pan on the stove and carefully added the garlic and herb paste. Once everything was combined and heated through, I allowed the mixture to cool slightly before brushing it onto the cut sides of the bread.

"Okay, that's ready to pop into the oven," I said as I slid the loaves cut sides up onto a baking sheet.

"Excellent," Grandma Jo said, deftly sliding a tray of meatballs out of the oven and popping the bread in. "The spaghetti noodles should be done right as the bread is ready. Thank you, Mikki. It looks and smells wonderful."

"Thank *you*, Grandma. I managed to not think about the bake off for about 15 whole minutes," I said. I sat down at the kitchen island, leaned my elbows on the counter, and rested my chin on my hands. "Grandma, why do we always have spaghetti and meatballs on Christmas Eve?"

Grandma Jo chuckled. "Well, when I was first married, it was the fanciest dish that I knew how to make. Plus, you have red sauce, and with a sprig of basil on top, you have your Christmas colors. And if you shave some Parmesan cheese on top, it looks like snow." She smiled with satisfaction. "And, it's an affordable meal that feeds a lot of people."

"I do love your spaghetti," I told her. I sighed and rubbed my temples. "This waiting is *killing* me. Do I have time for a walk before dinner's ready?" I asked.

Grandma Jo shook her head. "I don't think so, honey. Everything should be ready in about five minutes or so. Why don't you set the table?"

I got up and started for the sideboard where the holiday plates were stored when my phone vibrated in my back pocket. My entire body went numb and my heart raced. I reached for my pocket and managed to fumble the phone out with shaking hands. I took a deep breath and looked at the screen. It was a FaceTime call from Michael. I was surprised but pleased as I hit the green button to accept the call.

Michael's handsome face popped up on the screen. "Mikki? Hi, have you heard anything?" His eyes searched my face anxiously through the phone.

"Hi," I said, "I haven't heard anything yet. It sounds like you haven't, either, huh?"

"Nope." There appeared to be medical items on the wall behind him.

"Where are you?" I asked. The screen bobbed as Michael crossed the room.

"I've got someone I'd like you to meet," he replied.

The phone swung around and I saw an older woman lying in a hospital bed. The bed had been slightly raised under her head and torso and she was propped up on several pillows. Her long blonde hair was touched with gray, and it had been carefully brushed and arranged around her shoulders. Her hands rested on top of the blankets that had been pulled up to her chest. Her eyes, pale blue like Michael's, were open, and at the sight of me on the screen, she smiled weakly. I heard Michael's voice from the side.

"Mom, this is Michaela Branson. Mikki, this is my mom, Rachel."

"Hello," I said, giving a little wave. "It's nice to meet you."

The woman, Rachel, gave an almost imperceptible nod. She rolled her gaze towards the spot where I assumed Michael was standing and her eyes rolled around and her hand flopped on the blankets. Michael came into view again.

"She wants me to tell you that she's very happy to meet you," he said. He swung the phone back to show his mother, and I gave her a big smile.

"Your kolacky is delicious, Mrs. Brandon," I told her.

She thrashed her hand around again.

"She wants you to call her Rachel," Michael's voice informed me.

"Your cookies are delicious, Rachel," I said.

A little smile crossed the woman's face, and she settled peacefully onto her pillows.

"You have a very talented son." Pride shone from her eyes. "Merry Christmas, Rachel," I said with another wave.

Michael swung the phone back to himself. "Would you text me if you get a call from the Culinary Channel people?" he asked.

"Sure, if you'll do the same," I told him.

He agreed. Behind me, Grandma Jo called out that dinner was ready.

"Sounds like you've got to go," Michael said. "Good luck, and Mikki …" he hesitated.

"Yes?" I prompted.

"Merry Christmas," Michael replied abruptly and the screen went dark.

I got the distinct feeling that he had intended to say something else, but I couldn't begin to imagine what. I shook it off and went to set the table, determined to enjoy the meal with my family.

*   *   *

After stuffing ourselves with spaghetti and meatballs and garlic bread, followed by a decadent chocolate cake, we settled down in the living room to watch the rest of Clark Griswold's mishaps with his "fun, old-fashioned family Christmas." I tried to concentrate on the movie, but I kept checking my phone. My mother snatched the device out of my hands.

"Mikki, for goodness sake, you won't make it ring by looking at it every ten seconds!"

"I know, Mom, but I can't help it," I said. I grabbed for the phone and my mom playfully held it aloft. My mother was tall, like my grandfather's side of the family. I had inherited my petite size from Grandma Jo. As my mom put the phone behind her back, it began to ring. Mom's eyes widened, and she quickly held the phone out to me.

I felt like I might be having a stroke as pins and needles flooded my entire body. All the breath whooshed out of my lungs. My hands trembled as I saw that it was an unfamiliar number. I had to swipe at the green button multiple times because I was shaking so badly that I had lost all feeling in my fingers.

"Hello," I rasped out. I cleared my throat. "This is Michaela." My heart was hammering in my chest and I had a white-knuckled grip on the phone.

"Hello, Ms. Branson. This is Candy from the Culinary Channel. I'm calling to inform you that you're one of the five finalists in the bake off. We will need you to be back at the tent tomorrow at 10 a.m. sharp for the announcement of the winner. Congratulations!"

"Uh, thank you. I'll be there," I managed to croak.

"Happy holidays!" Candy said merrily. The line cut off, and the phone slipped from my grasp and bounced off the couch and onto the floor. My mother bent to pick it up as my father came in from the kitchen, wiping his hands on a towel.

"Dishes are done," he announced. "Was that the contest people on the phone?" he asked. "I thought I heard a phone ring."

"Yeah, Dad, it was the people from the bake off. I made it into the top five." I collapsed onto the couch and buried my face in my hands. "I can't believe it," I said, my voice muffled by my fingers.

"Oh, Mikki, I knew you could do it!" Grandma Jo cried, jumping up from her recliner.

I was buried in hugs and congratulations. "Don't get too excited, guys," I warned, "I haven't won anything yet."

My mother flapped her hand. "Darling, that's just a formality. We know you're going to win it all tomorrow!"

"Thanks, Mom," I said, beaming at her as she handed me my phone. I shot a quick identical text off to Michael and to Lacey. *I just got the call, I made the top five.* Lacey immediately replied with a high five emoji and a party hat emoji.

"Well, this calls for some eggnog," Grandma Jo announced. My mom laughed and followed her into the kitchen. "Then we should open our gifts!"

"Randall," she called over her shoulder, "let's do our scene from *A Christmas Carol* after we have eggnog."

My dad replied with a salute.

*   *   *

Halfway through my parents acting out the scene of Ebenezer Scrooge being visited by the Ghost of Christmas Future, my text alert dinged. I glanced at the phone. It was a text from Michael, only two words. *I'm in.*

I smiled and texted back. *Congrats, see you tomorrow.*

He replied with a smiling and winking emoji. Not, I noticed, the smiling winking emoji blowing a kiss.

Feeling a bit disgruntled, I watched my parents, each playing multiple parts, perform the rest of the scene. I applauded dutifully even though I hadn't been able to focus on the performance. My parents took their bows, and we all had another slice of cake before we passed around and opened our gifts.

I received a nice haircare set, a gorgeous chef's knife in its own carrying case, and my own mortar and pestle from

Grandma Jo. I had gifted her with several skeins of fancy silk thread and a bottle of her favorite lavender hydrosol. My parents always picked up interesting items on their travels, and I gasped with pleasure as I opened a handmade jeweled hair comb, dangling earrings in the shape of cats, and a colorful silk scarf. Everyone was pleased and grateful for their gifts.

I yawned as I stuffed the last of the wrapping paper into the recycling bin. "I had better turn in," I said. "I need to try and get some sleep so I don't look like a zombie on camera tomorrow."

"I'm tired," Grandma Jo said. "It was a long day. Good, but long. I'm ready for bed as well."

My parents concurred, and we all trooped off to our respective rooms.

My mind raced with thoughts of how winning could change my life. I would be able to pay off my student loans, freeing up a lot of monthly income. I would be able to start taking steps to open my own brick-and-mortar bakery. Maybe I could even upgrade to a nicer apartment, and I could certainly use a better car.

As I brushed my teeth, I stared into the mirror. I realized that all my goals involved myself. I hadn't given a thought as to how I might be able to help someone else with the money. I knew my parents were happy as clams with their nomadic theater life. My grandmother lived contentedly in her house and made a good living with her quilting skills. I was so fortunate to be blessed with a happy and healthy little family. Unlike Michael. All he really had was his mother, and she was in the hospital. But she was only in the hospital until her benefits ran out completely.

I climbed into bed and slipped under the padded quilt. Acorn jumped up and curled up against my side.

"Hey, boy," I said, rubbing him behind the ears. His purring comforted me. "Oh, Acorn. I really want to win, but I'll admit that I might feel more than a little guilty if I do. After all, I'm young and healthy and I have my whole life to reach my goals."

Acorn purred harder.

"I know, you're right. Fate will decide who wins tomorrow. I need to be content with that." But thoughts kept drifting through my mind—Michael's soft sobs, the sweet smile on his mother's face, my stiflingly boring job and my student loan balance and my bald tires. I reached over and turned off the bedside lamp. Acorn's purrs soothed my jumbled mind, and I finally drifted into a fitful sleep.

*   *   *

The next morning, I woke to my father singing "We Are the Champions" in his robust tenor voice. I smiled despite my grogginess and stretched. I checked my phone and was surprised to discover that it was after seven. I got up and headed for the shower, humming the Queen song on the way.

When I entered the kitchen, my family was seated at the table sipping coffee and talking. I joined them, gratefully pouring coffee into a mug from the carafe on the table.

My grandmother pushed a rack of toast and some butter and jam my way. "Good morning, dear. Merry Christmas! Have some toast. You'll need something in your stomach."

I sighed and began slathering butter on a piece of the toasted bread.

"You look lovely as always this morning, darling," my mother said, eyeing my red blouse and white cardigan. I had paired the top with dark-washed jeans and my boots. I had left my hair down and curled it on the ends a bit. I felt safer somehow with my hair around my face.

"Thanks, Mom. Merry Christmas," I mumbled around the toast.

"It's been one for the books, that's for sure," Grandma Jo said. "We should leave soon for the tent. It's after nine."

"Mother, the tent is all of ten minutes away," my mom protested. "Let's enjoy our morning."

"Ellen, you know that the traffic will be insane. The festival is in full swing today. They'll be lighting the tree on the town square."

"Right, I forgot," my mother responded, and she tipped her mug back to polish off her coffee. "And I assume you have to get fitted with your mic and everything, Mikki."

I shrugged and said, "I suppose so."

"By the way," my mother said, "who is that *gorgeous* man that was in the lineup with you yesterday?"

I blushed furiously. "Oh, uh, his name is Michael, he works at the coffee shop in town."

"Mmm-mmm, if only I were a younger woman," my mom teased, winking at my dad as he kissed her hand. They weren't fooling anyone. I knew that my parents adored one another. I laughed at their antics in spite of myself.

"Grandma's right, we need to go soon."

It felt like deja vu as we piled into the Jeep once again to head to the tent. I felt the butterflies alternating with the nausea again. "Dad, what's that technique you mentioned? Before you go on stage?"

My dad turned to me, clearly delighted that I had asked for his advice. "Well, I do some vocal exercises first, then I plant my feet on the ground and picture roots like a tree, anchoring me into the earth through the bottoms of my feet. Then I take deep, even breaths, counting to four on the inhale, hold for four, exhale to the count of four, hold for four, and start the cycle again. I do that until I feel calm and centered."

I ignored the vocal exercises, since I wouldn't be performing, and concentrated on the grounding and the breathing. By the time we pulled into the parking lot at the tent, I felt much calmer and more centered. Once again, we all parted as I headed for the contestant's entrance.

Along the way, I spotted Colleen heading towards the spectator's entrance. She gave me a wave and a watery smile. I assumed that she hadn't made the top five. I waved back, and she gave me a thumbs up. I looped my badge over my head as I moved through the entrance, carefully pulling my hair out from under the lanyard. The usual security guard lifted a hand in greeting as I passed.

I saw Carly attaching a wire to Michael's chest. His sweater was hiked up under his arms and my breath caught at the sight of his bare torso. He was beautifully sculpted, with a thin stripe of blond hair down the middle of his chest. I took it all in with appreciation, disappointed that Carly was so quick at her job.

I stepped up after Michael as he greeted me briefly and strolled away. While Carly attached my mic pack to my blouse, I noticed another man and two women that I didn't recognize waiting behind me. They must be the remaining contestants in the top five. Carly finished connecting me, with a reminder of how to turn the pack off and on.

"Okay, all set. Head on over to the north end of the tent, where the judging table is located. You'll see blue tape making X marks on the floor. Take your place on an X and the crew over there will give you further instructions."

"Thanks," I said, and headed away, making sure that the mic was in the off position. I had lost all the calm that I had built up in the car on the way over. I was back to shaking, extreme butterflies and nausea in my stomach, and a pounding heart. As I approached the area of the judge's table, I saw that Michael was there, standing stiffly on the first X. He looked at me with a small smile as I took my place on the second X on the floor.

"Good morning," he said.

"Hello," I said, staring straight ahead as I tried to stop the room from spinning. A member of the crew came up and told us that as soon as the remaining contestants were in their places, the judges would assemble and Ladd Bianchi would open the broadcast and the announcement would be made.

I stood on my place marker and tried to focus on my breathing, but it wasn't working. I saw white spots floating in front of my eyes and my stomach pitched violently. I clasped my hands over my mouth.

Michael turned to me. "Mikki, are you okay?" he asked, reaching out to steady me as I swayed.

"I think I'm going to be sick!" I managed to get out before I ran off the set. I ran blindly towards the outer edge of the tent, looking frantically for the nearest restroom or trash can. I spotted a door and stumbled through it. It was a little room with a table, not a restroom.

I plowed into the table in my mad rush, knocking a tray to the floor. I saw a big industrial trash can in the corner and ran to it. After heaving for a few minutes, my stomach decided to hold onto the toast and coffee after all.

Breathing deeply, I looked around for some water. I noticed that there were three envelopes on the floor where I had knocked the tray down. I went to pick them up and straighten out the mess I had made. The envelopes were labeled "Third," "Runner-Up," and "First Prize." In my haste, I had not only knocked the tray and envelopes to the floor, I had knocked the cards out of the envelopes. I was mortified that someone would come in and see what had happened and assume that I was trying to cheat or peek.

I quickly knelt and grabbed the tray and gathered the envelopes, intending to not look at the cards, but the "First Prize" and "Runner Up" envelopes were empty. I saw two cards lying face down on the floor. I gingerly knelt and picked them up. One card was labeled with Michael's name, and the other bore my name. I had no idea which card had been in which envelope.

I thought that I should probably just admit my mistake and let the crew put them back the way they were intended to be, but I was afraid that would disqualify the results. I thought about what winning would mean to me, and what it would mean to Michael.

As I debated what to do, I heard footsteps approaching the door to the room. I made my decision. I shoved the cards into the envelopes, threw everything back onto the tray, rushed behind the trash can, and squatted down. The door opened, and the footsteps entered, paused, and receded. I heard the door open and close again. I counted to twenty and slipped out of the room to head back to my spot at the judge's table.

I slid into place just as the judges were taking their seats. Michael looked at me out of the corner of his eye. "Are you okay? Where did you go?"

"I'm okay. I thought I was going to be sick, but it was a false alarm," I said.

"Quiet on set!" a man shouted. We turned to face the judges. The same man shouted, "And in three-two-one, action!"

Ladd Bianchi strolled out, wearing a green Hawaiian shirt with a pattern of multi-colored Christmas lights all over it. His trademark wraparound mirror sunglasses were perched on the back of his head.

"Welcome back, folks, and Merry Christmas to all. We're coming to you live from Pinewood Corners with the final five contestants in the Lights by the Lake holiday festival cookie bake off." Ladd turned to the lineup of contestants. He stepped in front of Michael. "What would you do with the grand prize winnings?" he asked.

"I would help out my mom," he replied.

"Aww, that's sweet. What a warm Christmas feeling that gives me," Ladd joked. Everyone laughed, and Michael looked a little embarrassed. Ladd moved on to me.

"Michaela, contestant 347, what about you? How would you spend fifty grand?"

"Well, Ladd, it's not too exciting. I would open a little bakery with whatever I had left after paying off my student loans," I said. Ladd raised his pierced eyebrows.

"Really? Well, that sounds prudent. You're right, it's kind of boring. Very nice, though." Everyone laughed again, and he moved on to the next contestant, who said that he would put it into his kids' college funds. The other two ladies wanted a new car and a remodeled kitchen, respectively.

Finally, Ladd announced that the time had come to reveal the winner.

"And as an added surprise," he paused for effect and continued, "the third place winner will receive the entire collection of Culinary Channel kitchen equipment and tools, carried exclusively at Bonner's Department Stores nationwide."

A murmur of excitement ran through the line of contestants.

"And the runner-up will receive ..." Ladd paused again and looked at each of us in turn. "Ten thousand dollars *and* the entire collection of Culinary Channel kitchen equipment and tools!"

Cheers erupted among the contestants and spectators. I was reeling. I had no idea there would be additional prizes for the runner-up and third-place contestants.

"Envelopes, please," Ladd said, holding out his hand. A crew member rushed up and handed the three envelopes to him. He shuffled through and selected one.

"In third place, winning the collection of chef quality tools and equipment from the Culinary Channel," he paused to open the envelope and extract the card. "It's contestant number 214, Jennifer Marks!" Music blared and the woman at the end of the line opposite Michael threw her hands in the air and began jumping up and down.

"Oh my gosh, that's me!" she screamed, rushing at Ladd and throwing her arms around him with such enthusiasm that she almost knocked him down.

"Whoa!" Ladd said, gently extracting himself, "If that's the reaction to third place, I'm a little frightened."

Everyone laughed again. The music stopped and silence descended once more.

"And now, the runner-up, winner of ten thousand dollars and the collection from the Culinary Channel, is—" he pulled the card out. "It's contestant number 347, Michaela Branson!"

I heard my grandmother whoop and my dad's piercing two-fingered whistle over the music. The room swayed, and I managed to feign a smile at Ladd and applaud as tears filled my eyes.

"Thank you so much," I stammered.

"And now, it's time for the grand prize winner to be revealed," he said dramatically, holding up the last envelope. I watched Michael's face as Ladd removed the card.

"The winner of the fifty-thousand dollar grand prize, and the chance to make their recipe on a Culinary Channel special, is none other than …" He paused and looked at the remaining contestants one by one. "It's Michael Brandon, contestant 447!"

Confetti rained down and the music kicked on again. Michael clasped his hands over his mouth as his eyes went huge in his face. I stood next to him, smiling from ear to ear.

"Oh my gosh, this is incredible!" Michael cried.

"Congratulations," I said, squeezing his hand. He surprised me by throwing his arms around me and giving me a hug that lifted me off my feet.

"Umph!" I mumbled, my face buried in Michael's shoulder. He grasped my shoulders and put me back on my feet and then vigorously pumped Ladd's hand.

"Congratulations, contestant 447, great job!" Ladd said to Michael. He then turned towards the camera closest to him.

"There you have it, folks. It's a very Merry Christmas for these contestants here today. Stay tuned for a highlight reel of the bake off and interviews with the winners and all the judges, coming up next right here on the Culinary Channel."

Someone yelled "Cut!" from somewhere and the lights went down and Ladd handed his mic off to an assistant. As he moved past me, he paused, studying me intently. I started to feel uncomfortable.

"Something wrong?" I asked, fidgeting under his gaze.

"Are you feeling better?" he asked. "I noticed that you were looking a little green around the gills when you ran off earlier." Before I could reply, Ladd continued. "I saw you run into the room where the envelopes were stored." He paused for my reaction and I felt my face redden as he continued. "Funny thing. I was the one who stuffed the envelopes before they were placed on that tray."

I gulped. "Please don't say anything. I, I …" I trailed off and Ladd tipped his head and studied me.

"I wouldn't call it cheating to take the lower spot. You wouldn't be the first person to throw a contest." He reached up and removed his sunglasses from the back of his head. "Have a great Christmas, Michaela. Congratulations again." He put on his sunglasses and strolled away. I released the breath I hadn't realized I was holding in a *whoosh*.

The spectators began to flood the contestant area, embracing and congratulating the winners, and consoling the two contestants that hadn't placed in the top three. My family fell on me, praising and hugging me. I saw the mayor clapping

Michael on the back, with a huge smile on his face. He said something I couldn't make out, then he turned to me.

"Congratulations, Mikki! Runner-up, that's wonderful!"

"Thank you, Mayor Reese, it's an honor," I replied.

"So much to celebrate," the mayor continued, "the contest, the festival, the holiday, and of course, the engagement announcement!"

My heart plunged to my toes as the edges of the room went dark. "Engagement announcement?" I asked. I didn't get a reply or an explanation, though.

More people flooded the area, and the music came back on as I was pulled along with the crowd and ended up on the outer edge near the door. I felt numb all over and yet my heart ached. I saw my parents speaking into a camera, loving the limelight as usual, and my grandma was over on the other side of the room with Sheriff Weaver. I had never felt so utterly alone, and I was surrounded by noise and people. I saw a camera and a clipboard minion headed my way.

Suddenly, I wanted nothing more than to be away from here. Away from this contest, away from the tent and all the joyful celebration, away from Pinewood Corners, and away from Michael Brandon.

Without thinking, I ripped off my mic, turned, and ran—past the security guard and out the front entrance. As I hit the parking lot, I realized that I had ridden here with Grandma Jo and my parents. I started to panic when a blue Ford sedan roared up. Lacey's bright auburn curls popped out of the driver's window.

"Get in," she ordered. "You look like you're about to pass out."

I trotted around and jumped into the passenger seat, slamming the door and leaning back with a sigh of relief as I fastened the seat belt.

"Claire's with Jed. I was late dropping her off, so I didn't get here until right before they made the announcement. I saw your face when Michael won. You *knew* he was going to win, didn't you?" Lacey glanced at me as she pulled onto Main.

"Yes, Lacey." I covered my face with my hands. "It was an accident. I thought I was going to be sick, and I was looking for a place to throw up, and I stumbled into the room where the envelopes with the winners were." I leaned forward, feeling nausea rising again.

"And then what happened?" Lacey prompted.

"And then I saw that I had knocked the contents out of the winner and runner-up envelopes," I said, pausing. "And then … and then I put Michael's card in the winning envelope."

"You what?" Lacey asked, looking at me. The car swerved, and she quickly placed her attention back onto the road.

"Well, he might have been the original winner, I don't know which card was in which envelope," I explained. I didn't tell her that Ladd Bianchi had admitted otherwise.

"That's true. And you did win ten grand," Lacey said. "What are you going to do now?"

"Now?" I asked. "Now I'm going to go home and continue with my life."

"What about Michael?" Lacey asked.

"What about him?" I said, trying to keep the bitterness out of my voice. "He'll do the same. He's got plenty to keep him busy now."

"What do you mean?" she asked as we pulled up in front of my grandmother's house.

"Just that he's happy now, and I'm not going to get in the middle of that," I said, turning to face her. "You saved my life back there. Thanks for the ride. I'll call you when I'm back home." I leaned across the seat and gave her a firm hug. I stepped out of the car and waved as the Ford pulled onto the road and drove away.

Chapter 16

The day after Christmas dawned gray and overcast. I woke up feeling groggy after driving through the night to get home. Acorn stretched and yawned on the pillow next to me.

"Good morning, sweetheart," I said, scratching him under his chin. I rolled over and checked my phone. There were texts from my parents and my grandma, beseeching me to call them, wanting to know why I had rushed off so quickly without saying goodbye, and telling me that they had some big news.

There were also multiple texts from Michael and two missed calls. He was asking me to call him. I promptly deleted the texts and blocked Michael's number. It was best to just make a clean break and let him get on with his life while I forged ahead with mine. I could admit to myself that I couldn't handle being just friends with Michael Brandon. It would be too painful. I sighed.

I supposed I should get calling my family over with, like ripping off a bandage. I hit the contact for Grandma Jo. She picked up on the first ring.

"Darling, where are you? Are you okay?" I assured her that I was home and that I was fine. I told her that I had just wanted to get home and settle in for a day before I had to go back to work at the resort.

"Well, you missed a wonderful party yesterday. We had quite the celebration," Grandma Jo informed me.

"I'm sorry, Grandma, but I didn't want a big fuss over me getting runner-up," I said.

"Well, Missy, the party wasn't entirely for you," Grandma Jo said. "Bob and I are engaged! He asked me on Christmas morning!" She sounded elated.

"Engaged?" *The engagement announcement.* Had I been mistaken? Then again, tons of people got engaged at Christmas. "Wow, that's wonderful, Grandma! Congratulations!"

"Thank you, Mikki-girl. We've set the date for this Valentine's Day!"

"Well, I guess I'll need to make another trip home really soon," I said.

"Bob and I decided that we didn't want to wait long. At our age, we know what we want," Grandma Jo said.

After some more conversation, and after speaking with my mom briefly, I hung up and marveled at my Grandma's news. I was genuinely happy for her. If my grandmother could find great love not once but twice, maybe there was hope for me, yet.

*   *   *

Two weeks later …

"Night, Stefan," I said as I climbed into my Chevy. Stefan grunted and turned to go back through the kitchen door. As I waited for my car to warm up, I checked my messages. I smiled at the texts from Grandma Jo, complete with pictures of antique wedding gowns asking me which I liked best.

I also had a couple of direct messages on my Instagram account inquiring about cookie orders. One customer was planning a baby shower and wanted two dozen cookies in a baby dinosaur theme with the message "Welcome Baby Malcolm" on them.

The second customer wanted six dozen cookies in a romantic theme, rose- and heart-shaped cookies. Whoa, six dozen was a big order for my little cookie business. I messaged back both customers with my price quote.

The baby shower was a month out, no problem, but the other customer wanted the romantic cookies in less than a week. If the customer agreed to my price, I would have to get busy right away.

To my surprise, my notification dinged almost immediately. The romantic cookie customer, whose username I didn't recognize, replied that the quote was agreeable, and that the money had been sent to me via Venmo already. The customer specified the time and location for the delivery and setup of the cookies. It was a fancy restaurant across town.

This person must really be trying to wow someone, I thought as I checked my Venmo account. Indeed, the money had already been sent. Impressed, I swung onto the road and headed for home, making a mental list of the baking supplies I would need to pick up tomorrow.

As the week went on, I managed to get the cookies designed and baked, and I finished off the decorating on the day of delivery. The cookies had come out beautifully, roses and hearts in various forms in shades of pinks and reds highlighted with rose gold and shimmering gold. I packed them carefully into boxes and loaded them into my car. I drove cautiously to avoid jostling the cookies too much.

The sun was setting as I pulled into the parking lot of the restaurant. I drove around to the side entrance, as instructed, and parked. I pulled my collapsible rolling cart out of the trunk and set it up. I loaded the boxes of cookies along with the display tiers onto the cart. I blew strands of stray hair that had escaped my messy ponytail out of my eyes and straightened my chef's jacket. I noticed that a few smears of frosting decorated the white jacket. I swiped at them but they were there to stay. With a shrug, I began rolling the cart towards the side door.

Once inside, it was so dim that I could barely see where I was going. *What's up with the lighting in this place?* I thought as I stumbled through the flickering candlelight in the private dining room. I moved directly to the massive sideboard along the edge of the room and began setting up my cookie display racks. I hummed as I worked, completely focused on the task at hand.

As I completed loading the displays, I turned around. Standing there in the flickering glow of the candlelight, holding a huge bouquet of roses and wearing a gray suit and a royal blue tie that set off his eyes, was Michael Brandon. Shocked to my core, I fell back against the sideboard, almost knocking over the displays that I had just set up.

"Michael!" I cried. "What are you doing here?" I felt all the air go out of my body in a rush and all feeling left my legs as I promptly sat down hard on the floor.

"Mikki, what are you doing? Are you okay?" Michael rushed over to me and knelt down, putting the roses on the sideboard behind me.

"What are you doing here?" I repeated. "I should go before she gets here," I said, struggling to get to my feet.

Michael gestured for me to stay put as he took a seat on the floor next to me. "Before who gets here?" he asked.

I leaned back against the sideboard for support. "Rayna. Isn't she meeting you here? Isn't that why you wanted the romantic cookie display?"

Michael reached out and ran a finger over my cheek. I shuddered as chills rolled over my entire body and every hair on my arms stood at attention.

"Mikki, Rayna and I are just friends. I work for her father, so I see a lot of her. I'm not interested in her. She's more like a sister or cousin to me. For me, she lacks ..." He paused. "Oomph. If that makes sense? I like a woman with character," he said softly.

I toyed nervously with the buttons on my chef's jacket. "So who are you here to meet?" I asked in a small voice.

Michael leaned forward and brushed his lips against my ear. "You," he whispered.

My heart leaped and plunged and danced in my chest and tears stung my eyes as I closed them.

"I can't get you out of my mind, Michaela Branson," Michael continued. "You are the most talented, passionate, interesting, funny, and intelligent woman I've ever met. When you left Pinewood Corners, I didn't know that you took my heart with you until I woke up every day feeling sad and disappointed when I remembered that I wouldn't get to see you that day. I missed spending time with you. I even missed your sarcasm."

He put a finger under my chin and raised my face to look at him. His smiling eyes gazed into mine. "And did I mention the most beautiful person, inside and out?" He passed a hand softly over my hair. "You wouldn't return my messages, so I placed a cookie order from the best baker in the state."

Tears spilled over as I gazed at him. "Oh, Michael, I don't know what to say—" I began.

"Say yes, Michaela. Say yes to a chance with me, a chance with *us*," he said, scooting closer to me. "You did a selfless thing, the most generous thing that anyone has ever done for me before."

I looked away at the floor. "I don't know what you mean. I—"

"I had a little chat with Ladd Bianchi. Lacey, too."

"Oh. Well, you know, I didn't know which was which. I just put them in the envelopes. The envelopes were on the tray, and I accidentally knocked the envelopes off the tray, and then the envelopes were empty, and I just put the cards back into the envelopes," I stammered. *Stop saying "envelopes!"* my mind screamed.

"I was able to get my mom into Briarwood, where she can get the care she needs," Michael said. "And I invested the rest in a building on Main Street that I'm turning into a bakery. I'll need a partner to help me run it."

"That's great," I said, gazing over at him. He looked so handsome in his suit, and I was suddenly conscious of my smudged jacket and messy ponytail. I began to fidget with my hair, but Michael reached up and gently grasped my wrist.

"No need to fix anything, you're gorgeous," he told me, drawing my wrist towards him and pulling me even closer to him. "I got you something," he reached up to one of the nearby tables and grabbed a gift bag that he handed to me. I reached in and pulled out a green apron with "MB Squared" embroidered on the top, and my tears began to flow in earnest.

"I love you, Michaela," he locked his gaze with mine and put his arms around me. "Say yes, say you'll give us a chance. I want you to be my baking partner from here on out. Say you'll move to Pinewood Corners and run the bakery with me."

He leaned forward, and our lips met in an earth-shattering kiss that melted my heart completely and poured it down into my toes. I let out a small sound of satisfaction as Michael pulled back to look into my face.

I could only respond with one simple word, but that word was enough.

"Yes," I said, and kissed him again.

Epilogue

The chill wind blew my hair into my eyes and I pushed it away as I gazed up at the sign affixed to the building over the front door. The sign was in green lettering, and it read "MB Squared Bakery and Cafe." Michael tightened his arm around my waist.

"This is amazing, Mikki," he said, his voice thick with emotion. "Our very own bakery. What do you think?"

I gazed up at him, struck at how he could still take my breath away with his square jaw and tumble of dark blond hair. "I am so proud and so happy, I keep pinching myself to make sure it's all real," I told him.

"If everything stays on track, we'll be able to open in time for the Sweetheart Soiree festival in mid-February," Michael said, giving me a light pinch to my upper arm.

I swatted at his hand with a grin and giggled. "That would be perfect. I've got some gorgeous Valentine's themed petit fours in mind that I'd love to try out."

"Sounds amazing," he replied, planting a kiss on the top of my head.

"I still can't believe that everything is happening so quickly," I marveled.

"Well, it helps to be acquainted with the town mayor," he said with a wink.

As we stood there, a blue Ford came rolling up and parked in the closest slot on the street. The driver's door opened and a petite, curvy redhead got out. "Hiya!" My best friend Lacey bounced up and gave me a firm hug. "How goes it with the pre-grand opening stuff?" she asked.

"It's going so smoothly, it's almost scary," I said.

Lacey laughed. "Don't be scared, chickadee, be grateful. You'll probably be ready to open in time for the Valentine's festival next month."

Michael's face lit up. "That's what I was just telling Mikki!"

Lacey looked up and scrutinized the building and she sighed. Her green eyes clouded over.

"What's wrong?" I asked her.

She shuffled her feet and a faint blush crept up her face, highlighting the smattering of freckles across her nose. "I don't want to say," she muttered.

I lowered my brows and gave her a stern look.

"Okay, okay," she groused. "It's just that the Sweetheart Soiree is so close, and seeing you two so happy together, and now that Jed is dating someone else—"

"Wait, what?" I cut her off. "I had no idea that Jed was seeing anyone. Is it serious? Is it anyone that I know?"

"It's Elaine Laramie, the pharmacy tech at Marcus Pharmacy. They've been going out for a couple of months now," Lacey replied. "Anyway, all of it has got me feeling kind of melancholy." She looked at me with wide eyes. "Not," she said, holding up one hand, palm out, "that I'm jealous or anything like that. I'm truly happy for you guys. But I can admit that I'm a little tired of Saturday nights spent watching the *Real Housewives of Wherever* alone on the couch after Claire goes to bed. Something a little more adventurous would be nice."

I nudged her playfully with my elbow. "With someone tall, dark, and handsome?" I teased.

Lacey threw back her head and laughed, red curls bouncing. "At this point, short, bald, and with a pulse will do," she said wryly.

"It can happen when you least expect it," Michael said, throwing his arm around my shoulders with a grin.

"In the meantime," I said, tongue firmly in cheek, "I'll keep my eyes peeled for any short, bald guys with a pulse and steer them your way."

Lacey smacked me lightly on the arm. "You will do no such thing. I'll find my own dates. Somehow. Maybe." She sighed again. "Anyway, the place looks great. I can't wait to become a regular customer. In the meantime, I'd better get going. The library won't open itself." She waved and hopped into her car and roared away.

I leaned my head on Michael's shoulder. "Do you think it will happen for her? That she'll find someone?" I asked him.

"Sure," he said, pulling me to his side. "Look at us. We didn't plan on meeting and falling in love. We weren't even looking for romance, and we fell into each other's laps."

I laughed. "Almost literally," I said, recalling our first meeting.

"Besides," Michael continued, "I'm convinced that the festivals in this town have magic in them, and the next festival is all about love and romance."

I tipped my head to the side and considered him. "Do you believe in magic?" I asked.

"Sure," he said, circling me within the warmth of his arms. "How else do you explain falling in love?" He leaned in and his kiss was devastating in the sweetest of ways as the snow began to fall around us.

The End

Will Lacey find someone special to spend her
Saturdays with? Find out in the next book in the
Pinewood Corners Sweet Romance series,
The St. Valentine's Situation.

Acknowledgments

I would like to extend my gratitude to my wonderful husband, Michael, for his continued support and unshakable belief in me, to my kids for sharing their social media prowess, my grandchildren for being such a joy, to my "yoga ladies" and my brunch crew for always being my cheering section, to my kind and caring publisher for her patient guidance, and of course, this book would not be complete without a 'nod' to my excellent editor, Lori.

About the Author

Carol Babineaux has always loved stories about love. She hails from the southwest desert now but has fond memories of the snowy holidays of her Ohio childhood, so she blended her memories and her passions together into her debut novel in the Pinewood Corners Sweet Romance series. Carol has enjoyed a long career in administration and has a diploma in Integrative Healing and Hypnotherapy from the Southwest Institute of Healing Arts. When she isn't writing, she can be found in yoga class, reading, cooking, watching movies, and spending time with family and friends. Carol lives in Arizona with her husband and a gaggle of cats.

carolbabineaux.com

www.ingramcontent.com/pod-product-compliance
Lightning Source LLC
Chambersburg PA
CBHW070505300726
48975CB00007B/2329